1

PLACES!

A Musical About a High School Theatre Group Producing a Musical About a High School Theatre Group Producing a Musical

by Lowery Christopher Collins

PLACES!

A Musical About a High School Theatre Group Producing a Musical
About a High School Theatre Group Producing a Musical

by Lowery Christopher Collins

PLACES!
A MUSICAL ABOUT A HIGH SCHOOL THEATRE GROUP PRODUCING A
MUSICAL ABOUT A HIGH SCHOOL THEATRE GROUP PRODUCIUNG A
MUSICAL

Written by Lowery Christopher Collins

Copyright © 2020 by Lowery Christopher Collins

Ponderlake Publishing: www.ponderlake.com

Playwright and/or Royalty Information: www.ChristopherCollinsOnline.com

ISBN 978-1-7349926-4-9

PLACES!

A MUSICAL BY L. CHRISTOPHER COLLINS

Cast of Characters

THE ADULTS

MALES	FEMALES
Evan Brighton	Margie
Mr. Stone	Diedre Malone Sanderson
Anton Sebowski	Ruby Riley
Edmond Charles	Serena Bradley
The Stage Manager	Caroline Adamson
	Cynthia Charles

STUDENTS

FEMALES	MALES
Crystal	Vince
Kara	Johnson
Olivia	Todd
Melody	Trent
Amanda	Ruben
Jade	Josh
Kate	Magnus
Kitt	Ian
	Logan
As many other students as are needed: Geena, Tina, Jenny, Sean, Tom, Piers, Paul, Mark, Greg, Lana, Vinicia, Ulysses, Ricky, etc.	Quinton
	Bryan
	Dakota
	TJ
	Cooper
	John David

12

PLACES!

A MUSICAL BY L. CHRISTOPHER COLLINS

#1--Prologue--Introductions –Music

PROLOGUE:

We hear a voice of authority announce "Places!" One by one, the characters walk downstage to address the audience. After a few seconds the lights come up on the various characters.

Vince

Can you believe that I'm here? Can you believe that I'm standing? I'm here before a crowd of friendly faces, all wishing me well. Well, hopefully. . .

Crystal

It's hard to believe that I'm here. I'm not shaking and quivering with stage fright? Much. I'm trying to stand here with confidence and with
a smile.

Johnson

I never thought I would be here, never thought I'd stand before you. I never had an urge to do this until I did. Now I'm hooked.

Kara

I'm in shock that I, too, am here. I've never been one to be . . .
open.
It's a big deal for me to be here, even standing.

Olivia

I know that I belong here. I've never been anywhere that feels as
right. I know that I am where I belong on this stage.

Todd

I used to make fun of people here. Standing up here and
performing.
I thought they were weak and light on their feet and just . . . you
know . . . strange. But now I'm here and I see why they do it. I now
know why they pursue it. Now that I'm here.

Trent

I wonder why I am here. Why I am doing this here and now? I know
I can pull this off, but do I want to?

Melody

I'm so happy that I am here again. I am standing in front of my
family,
all the people who care enough to drive out here and see us.

Ruben

Well, as you can see, I'm here. I'm standing on stage, and I'm
turning a page on my life.

Josh

You may ask yourself why I'm here. Why would I spend time in this
place? I'll probably end up as a lawyer or doctor or teacher or
something much different, but why am I doing this here? It's
because . . .

Kara

What I am doing right here, right now, this moment, this second,
this time, this place, this prep, this sweat, these tears, this

everything here is helping me be who I need to be, grow how I need to grow, face all my demons, relating with others, learning and changing and speaking and trying and hoping to grow.

Magnus

I know why I'm here.

Ian

I know why I'm here.

All

Everyone repeats his/her previous line and ends with

I WANNABE

Eventually, sing in a rotation.

I WANNABE I WANNABE I WANNABE HERE!

I'M HERE!

This leads into the melody of "Play the Part"

ACT I

ACT I, SCENE 1

#2--Background to Margie and the Group –Music

Margie, a custodian enters from down stage left.

Margie

So. Here we are. The stage. The stage. This magical place. Don't get me wrong: I'm not a theatre person. No, not me. But I've been

15

here. I've seen a few things, well, I've seen just about everything. And seeing just about everything changes a person. No, I'm not a teacher. And (laughs) heavens no, not a student. Heck, maybe a hundred years ago. I help take care of this building. I have an entire wing to myself, and I make sure it is spotless, well, as spotless as some of this rooms CAN be. I vacuum and dust and mop and straighten and do just everything I can to make sure these kids and these teachers have a good environment. But this group. My, oh, my. This group. And that man. I was here ten years ago when he showed up, and I've seen what can be. Like I said, I ain't no theatre person. I never did anything like that, and to be honest, I'd never really seen it, either. But ten years ago, I noticed something gradual. Sure, to some people those people are wild and weird and well, bouncy, but they weren't the bad seed I'd thought of all my life. These people were mannerly and kind, and . . .

A few break the "freeze."

Crystal

Hey, Margie.

Margie

Hey, girl.

Dakota

Margie, how are you?

Margie

Hello, Dakota, I am fine. Just taking care of business. How are you?

Dakota

I'm great, Margie.

Ian

Yo, ho, ho, Miss Margie.

Margie

And a bottle of rum, mate!

Margie

Yes, a little weird still. I've watched them. I've gone to their shows. And yes, I have cleaned and listened to classes and rehearsals. And I can't retire now, because I want to see what happens next. This is something I've learned. What you see behind you is called a "tableau." It's a frozen picture on a stage. Watch. Now.

Snaps fingers. Action resumes. Snaps fingers again. Tableau resumes.

See. It comes in handy. I picked that up from Mr. Brighton. You may ask how I am able to do that. It's not magic. It's just that what you see behind you is not happening right now. This entire musical is a recent memory. Everything you're about to see just happened in recent memory. And it was definitely the building up of a lot of things, people, events, and everything else you can remember. Some years are just tension years as I call them, or at least everything just comes to a head. But it's more than the story of a group of performers. It's more than the story of a school. I watched while this became the story of a community and of a people. Yes, I watch. I watch as people of all ages grow and learn and as we all change. This is the most fun part of my job. And you know, I was wrong about what I said earlier. I AM a theatre person. Once you know what that means, we all are.

Tableau breaks.

Mr. Brighton walks by busy.

Evan

Good morning, Margie.

Margie

Good morning, Mr. Brighton. How's the room looking today for you?

Evan

It was sparkling, and it smelled like lemons, Margie. Thank you.

Margie

I aim to please, Mr. Brighton. I aim to please.

They both leave stage, busy.

Trent

Ian, you work this afternoon?

Ian

Yeah. I have to be there at 4 today. We have a shipment to unload.

Trent

Okay. when you get off, stop by the house. My dad bought me a new guitar.

Ian

For real?

Trent

For real.

Olivia

Hey, you auditioning tomorrow or Friday?

Vince

Both, if he'll let me.

Olivia

Both? There are too many people on that list. Do you think he'll . . .

Vince

Yes.

Olivia

Yes, he will.

Josh

Amanda.

Amanda

Yes.

Josh

Are you having a good day?

Amanda

It's okay. Why do you ask?

Josh

Want to have a good evening?

Amanda

Maybe.

Jade

What time is your game tonight?

Todd

5:30

Jade

Have one tomorrow night?

Todd

No, but we do have practice until 7, which means . . .

Jade

You're auditioning Friday instead.

Todd

Yeah. I have to see if he can see me at an earlier time.

Logan

Why are you so flippin' weird?

Quinton

Leave me alone.

Logan

Buy a new pair of pants.

Quinton

Buy another friend.

Kara

My mom just took a third job. I'm worried. And she won't let me work.

Bryan

At all?

Kara

Nope. School, school, school.

Bryan

But.

Kara

I know. I know. I love her so much.

Melody

Did you finish the costume project?

Dakota

Before or after the chemistry?

Melody

Well . . .

Dakota

Before or after the Pre-Cal?

Melody

You . . .

Dakota

Before or after the Canterbury Tales essay?

Melody

If you . . .

Dakota

Before or after studying for the WW II exam?

Melody

I, uh . . .

Dakota

Of course, I finished it, are you crazy?

Melody

Cool.

Josh

Well, hello.

Kate

Josh. Joshie. Josh.

Josh

Kate. Katie. Kate. Were you smiling at me in the snack line today?

Kate

I have a natural smile, Josh.

Josh

That you do. That you do.

Kate

Mr. Straight A's, did you finish the homework for Phillips?

Josh

Done.

Kate

Could I?

Josh

Sure. Come on.

Vince

You ready?

Crystal

I'm ready!

3--TO PLAY THE PART --SONG

VINCE

WE EACH WALK UPON A STAGE TO FIND THE LIGHT.
AND WE TRY TO FIND THE PLACE THAT FEELS RIGHT.

CRYSTAL

FOR WE EACH MUST PLAY OUR PART
TO MAKE OUR WORLD A BETTER PLACE.
AND WE WORK ALL THROUGH OUR DAY INTO THE NIGHT
TO PLAY OUR PARTS.

IAN

WE GREET THE WORLD EACH SINGLE DAY WITH ALL THAT WE CAN
DO

TRENT

AND WE CLASSIFY THE TALENTS THAT WE BRING

JOHNSON

WE USE THE TRUTH WE KNOW ON OUR PATHWAY AS WE GO.

EVAN

AND WE EACH HAVE A DIFFERENT SONG WE SING.

ALL

We play the part! We play the part!
We each have a different purpose from the start.

JOSH

Some take the lead. And some succeed to
focus on the smaller roles with gumption and with
heart.

ALL

We live the role with mind and soul
And no matter what our calling
or how life make take its toll
We do create a face to meet the faces that we meet.
We do what we must do.
And we hope that we'll stay true
We do create a face to meet the faces that we meet.
We do what we must do.
And we hope that we'll stay true
To the honesty and privilege that we have
To play the part.

OLIVIA

Some care for young and old.
Some labor through the heat and cold.

RUBEN

Some sacrifice their dreams
to put some food upon the plate.

MELODY

Some lead a winning team.
Some clothe the world with stitch and seam.

LOGAN

But every single person has a future to create.

JADE

WITH CHOICES TO BE MADE
WE DEFINE THE ROLES THAT MUST BE PLAYED
WE MAY BE ON A STAGE
OR JUST A STAGE WITHIN OUR LIVES

EVAN

BUT IF THE TRUTH BE TOLD
WE CREATE THE ROLES THAT DO UNFOLD
AND WITHIN THIS PART,
WE FIND THE COURAGE TO SURVIVE!

ALL

WE PLAY . . .

OH, WE PLAY THE PART!
WHAT AN AMAZING TASK WE HAVE!
TO NOT ONLY ACT
BUT ACT WITH STRENGTH OF COURAGE AND OF TRUTH.
WE CHOOSE TO REMEMBER WHO WE ARE!
AND NEVER SACRIFICE OUR SOULS TO WHOM WE WISH TO BE!!

ACT I, SCENE 2

A group is acting out a scene from an "average play." There is no energy. Mr. Evan Brighton is at the back of the room, watching, letting Melody lead.

Melody

Act it out, people! I can't believe this.

Olivia

Are you kidding me? You guys have been doing scenes for
years, and this is the . . .

Melody

Olivia. Olivia. I can handle it.

Olivia

I know, but these . . .

Melody

Liv. I know. I know.

Olivia

Okay. It's just that . . . okay.

Melody

I know.

Ruben

If I'm going to be yelled at, I'm not doing this. I can sit down.

Melody

Ruben.

Ruben

I'm not joking.

Melody

Ruben, it's okay. It's just that you have to act. You know how
to act. I've seen you act. I've acted with you. I just can't feel it.
It's not happening. Make it happen. Make it click. Make me
believe you.

Ruben

You enjoy repeating everything Mr. B always tells us?
Mr. Brighton, do you hear her?

Melody

See. I'm just telling you what you already know.

Ruben

Mr. B? Help me here.

Melody

He put in charge of this activity. I'm directing this if you don't mind.

Olivia

There we go.

Ruben

Mr. B!

Evan

Yes, Ruben?

Ruben

Do you hear her?

Evan

I do. She's giving you a hard time, isn't she?

Ruben

Mr. B., I know where you're going with that, but . . .

Evan

Ruben?

Ruben

Yes, sir?

Evan

What's the role of the director?

Ruben

Mr. B. . . .

Evan

Ruben.

Ruben

To make decisions about the acting, blocking, atmosphere, tempo, mood, and flow of the production.

Evan

And is that what Melody's doing?

Ruben

But she . . .

Evan

Is that what she's doing?

Ruben

Yes, sir.

Evan

Thank you. Now, it's our job as actors to take direction.

Melody

Thank you!

Evan

But.

Olivia

Listen to this.

Melody

Crap.

Evan

It's the duty of director to be cordial and professional and to keep in mind the way in which to inspire the actors, not merely to be the boss. An actor needs concrete suggestions, not just broad orders.

Ruben

Thank you.

Evan

Melody, can we try this again?

Melody

Yes, sir. (*Pause.*) Ruben.

Ruben

Yes, Melody.

Olivia

That's what I'm talking about.

Evan

Olivia?

Olivia

I'm shutting up.

Melody

I need to see that your character . . . cares about what's happening here.

She looks back at Mr. Brighton. He nods.

Ah. When she called you, it looked like, uh, that you didn't hear what she was saying. She is telling you something you don't want to hear. What would a person do, how would a person look if he were upset by a phone call? It's a bad call. It's one that really, really bothers you. How would you react to being told something that infuriated you?

Ruben

You want a physical move? A fist through the wall?

Melody

No, more of a restrained anger. Yeah, like you WANT to put a fist through the wall, but you think about your potential broken hand and decide against it. So, you, uh, show me that, yeah. . . you show me on your face that you are thinking about a fist through the wall. But you let the audience know by your looking at your fist and your facial expressions that you're even more angry that you cannot find an outlet for your anger so it boils on your face. Does that make sense?

Ruben

Yeah. Let me try it.

He acts out this scene, hanging up the phone, acting upset, and it works.

Olivia

Look at you, Ms. Spielberg.

Logan

That's wasn't bad.

Jade

(Obviously with a crush on Logan)
Not at all. Not bad. Logan's right.

Evan

Good scene, guys. Ruben, believable. Excellent. Mel, you found what he could relate to and used his own suggestion and ran with it. Mature decision. Let's circle around, guys, and talk about auditions.

The door opens. Tom Jefferson Keller, HS junior, walks in accompanied by a high school counselor.

Sebowski

Hello, Mr. Bright, class.

Evan

Well, hello, Mr. Sebowski. Welcome to the green room.

Sebowski

The green room? Oh, yes. Sorry I didn't knock. I did see the "knock first" sign. As a counselor and academic coordinator at Legacy Road High, I see signs, but I don't always respond. Anyway. I came on in.

Trent

Where'd that come from?

Ian

Senility. Ignore it.

Evan

It's no problem. What can I do for you?

Sebowski

Do for me? Oh, yes. Yes. We have a new student here at Legacy Road High, and he's enrolling in your class.

Evan

Very good.

Sebowski

His name is Thomas Jefferson Keller.

TJ

TJ.

Evan

(Looks at schedule)
Thomas Jefferson Keller.

TJ

TJ.

Evan

Of course. TJ.

Several Students

Hello, TJ, Hey, What's up? etc.

Evan

Welcome to the green room, TJ. Just find a place to sit. We're talking about a few important things.

Sebowski

On that bittersweet note, I'll go find a new hummingbird to nest.

Johnson

Did he say "hummingbird"?

Logan

Yeah. To nest.

Johnson

Wow.

Logan

Learn to live in amazement.

Jade

(*Giggling*) Amazement.

Sebowski

Mr. Keller, again, welcome to Legacy Road High School, one of the best schools in the state, where our unofficial motto is 'We might as well be private.' Toodaloo, students. Carry on.

Sebowski leaves the room.

Evan

We have auditions for our comedy coming up in a very few days.

Crystal

Where are the sign-up sheets, Mr. B?

Bryan

(*Rubbing hands together in anticipation*) Let's do this!

Dakota

You're torturing us here.

Vince

We have to get the good slots ASAP. I don't wanna audition too early before everyone else, and I don't want to go on at midnight, either. It's strategy, people.

Evan

TJ, we take our theatre pretty seriously here.

TJ

Evidently.

Kara

It's our thing. Go with it.

Todd

Were you in theatre in your last school?

TJ

No.

Todd

Really?

TJ

Well, I did I little bit when I was younger when my dad wanted me to. He's into it a lot, and since I am living with him now, he wants me in here.

Ian

Good dad. Good dad! Ah, well, welcome to the company, man. Welcome! You're in the best of the best.

TJ

I'm in something.

Ian

Aw, don't worry. Most people think it's a bit weird when they know nothing about it. Once you're in it, you realize how great it is.

TJ

(*Unenthusiastically*) Okay.

Evan

Leave him alone, guys. It's tough being a newcomer to something.

TJ

I'm okay. Really.

Evan

Good. Back to sign ups. I put them up later to make it fairer. It's first-come, first-serve time slots, but it has to be accessible at a fair time: today at 2:30, between the last two classes. That's your heads up. I expect a good number of you sign.

Trent

Don't worry. You'll have a full slate.

ACT I, SCENE 3

Margie

(*Startled*) Whoa. (*The class freezes. She looks over at young lady who has appeared next to her.*) You scared the life out of me. Who are . . . Oh, my Lord. Diedre? Diedre Malone!

Diedre

Well, it's "Sanderson" now. Hello, Margie. (*They hug.*) How are you?

Margie

Good, my dear. (*to audience*) This is one of the products, one of the kids here the first year: Diedre Malone.

Diedre

(*Smiling*) Sanderson. And far from a kid. I have little ones myself now.

Margie

Fair enough. Sneaking up on my memory?

Diedre

Just seeing what's happened in recent years and adding another perspective to the production.

Margie

This is the . . .

Diedre

I heard. I see. And this was the moment that things pivoted?

Margie

This opened the scene.

Diedre

Wow. I remember Bright when he first got here. I didn't get the full four with him. He came when I was a junior, and everything begin to explode, in a good way of course.

#5--Background--Susan and the Years –Music

Margie

I remember.

Diedre

But things exploded in a not-so-good way, too. Susan.

Margie

Oh, yes. Susan.

The students all reorganize the classroom in a traditional seating. They also put on white, faceless masks. Diedre joins them as a student. Mrs. Sebowski enters.

Sebowski

Students, I bring you very sad news today. As you can probably tell from his absence, Mr. Bright is unable to be here today. I don't know if you were aware, but he has been engaged to be married.

Jade

To Ms. Green.

Sebowski

So, he has spoken of her?

Johnson

Yes, sir. We've actually met her.

Olivia

What happened?

Sebowski

That makes it all the more difficult. Susan Green and two of Mr. Bright's other friends were in a terrible automobile accident last night. None of them survived.

The students react randomly with concern.

Sebowski exits. Diedre removes her mask and speaks to Margie.

Diedre

We didn't know what to expect after that. Depression, anger, even his leaving. But it was something different.

Bright walks into the classroom. As he speaks, students, one-by-one, begin removing their masks.

Evan

I want to thank you for your concern and for the flowers. You've shown me what you're made of. Maybe, I can see what I'm made of. Yes, I am most certainly a mess right now. And no, I can't talk about it with you really. I don't know what to say other than what I'm saying. I do know that life is much shorter than I ever realized. And I know it's not for the weak or the indecisive. You have to work for joy. And work is exactly what I plan to do. Sit in a way that I can see you all better.

The students, now unmasked, break from the traditional seating.

Diedre

And work, we did. I was involved in the first few.

As Diedre and Margie begin naming productions, the students create obvious tableaus, sometimes funny, from the specific shows. There has to be time between the plays in the list for the tableaus to be formed.

Evan

Places!

Diedre

Romeo and Juliet. The Crucible. Private Lives. Grease. Arsenic and Old Lace. The Fantasticks. West Side Story.

Diedre joins Margie and watches.

Margie

And kids come and go. *Noises Off. The Elephant Man. A Streetcar Named Desire. The Man of La Mancha. You're a Good Man, Charlie Brown. Forever Plaid. Waiting for Godot. The Sound of Music. The Importance of Being Earnest. Agnes of God. Hamlet.* And more.
The years have come and gone, and we all keeping going along. I'm happy to say that I have seen every one of them.

The students stand upstage with their backs to the audience.

ACT I, SCENE 4

Diedre

(*to Margie*) But you're telling me that something changed?

Margie

Something subtle. Something even Mr. B. didn't see coming at first.

The original class resumes (at the point at which Evan has finished discussing auditions).

Evan

And if you'll be sure to sign up for auditions as soon as you can this afternoon, I can make sure there are no conflicts. Now, something you've all been waiting for: this year's contest play information. *(The excitement in the room intensifies. TJ notices.)* I got all the specifications and the category yesterday afternoon.

Crystal

Yesterday?

Logan

And you didn't tell us?

Evan

I still have a few secrets.

Melody

From us?

Evan

Especially from you guys.

Vince

Oh, Mr. Bright. Say it ain't so!

Evan

I cannot tell a lie.

Todd

So, tell us. What's the category?

Ruben

What is it?

TJ

Category of what?

Vince

This year's official contest. Every year, we enter the official state theatre contest. Each year it's a different set of rules. Last year, it was a modern tragedy, written by students, paralleling a anything by Euripides.

Trent

Year before, it was any farce written by an American playwright.

Johnson

Year before that . . .

Melody

I think he gets it. Okay, Mr. B., enough stalling.

Josh Gardner enters.

Josh

Hey, hey, Company B.

A few say hello in return but quickly set their sights back on Evan, who has information they want.

Jade

So, Mr. B.

Evan

Where have you been, Josh?

Josh

Dentist. Got the note and all. On the up-and-up.

Evan

I believe you.

Olivia

You always do.

Evan

As I do with you.

Vince

So, Mr. B

Josh

What are you guys drilling Bright for?

Todd

This year's contest category.

Josh

Already?

Melody

It *is* October, Josh.

Josh

So it is. So, Mr. B. What do we have?

Evan

Well, you all know the rules.

Logan

60 minutes tops. Simple set.

Jade

(Referring to Logan) He knows his rules.

Crystal

Costumes must be student-made.

Melody

No fewer than five nor more than twenty students.

Several Students

What's the category?

Evan

A musical about your life.

Vince

YES!!

Logan

A musical??

Evan

Well, you all know the rules.

Kitt

A musical?

Crystal

About our lives?

Josh

About my life?

Jade

Have they ever asked for a musical before?

Evan

Not since I've been doing this.

Olivia

A Musical???

Vince

Not about Nazis or AIDS or Huck Finn?

Trent

About our lives.

Evan

A musical about your life.

Vince

YES!!

Logan

You love musicals, don't you?

Vince

Yes. (*Smiles*)

Johnson

Can we do this?

Ian

Of course, we can do this.

Josh

We're Company B.

TJ

You guys are going to write a musical? And perform it?

Josh

Who is this?

Olivia

This is Thomas Jefferson Keller. New kid.

Ian

TJ

Josh

Well, new kid, to answer your question, yes. Yes, we are. We always do what is asked of us. We don't always win, but it's always a hell of an experience along the way

Evan

We always give it our best shot, and we are always remembered. That's sometimes better than any trophy.

The bell rings.

Remember auditions and try to think of ideas for the contest piece. I know some of you have lunch now. I have some beginning actors coming in now for improv. If you choose to stay, find a place to plant yourself.

A few students leave, but most move to the side and sit. TJ starts to go but stops, sits, and watches. As the new students enter, one or two girls touch and flirt with Josh. TJ notices.

Margie freezes the action.

Margie

This is where TJ got hooked. Just look at him. He was amazed that these kids were excited about something he'd never thought as exciting.

Diedre

I guess he was expecting a group of nerds and wimps?

Margie

That isn't what he found. Watch.

Margie snaps the play back into action a few minutes down the road. Party Quirks. Everyone claps

Evan

I hope you new guys don't mind, but whenever I mention improv, a lot of my old hats around here can't stay away. We definitely have some hams around here. NOW, I need some of you newbies to volunteer. Come on. A simple activity. Let's try Returns.

Cooper

I'll try.

John David

So will I.

Evan

Very good. Let's see. Simple scenario. Cooper, step outside for a few seconds.

Cooper steps out.

Evan

OK, John David, Cooper doesn't know it, but he is returning a mop. You have to hint at what he has, but never give it away. Keep acting the whole time.

John David

OK.

Logan gets Cooper and brings him back inside.

Evan

OK. You know the drill. You have an item that you are returning. John David knows what it is, but you actually don't. As he talks with you, you have to try to figure out what you are returning.

Cooper

Got it.

Evan

Good. Places. Go.

John David

Hello. May I help you?

Cooper

Yes. I need to return this whatever it is.

Evan

Come on, act. Pretend you do know what it is.

Cooper

I have this thing that I need to return.

John David

What sort of thing is it?

Melody

You know.

Evan

Melody.

John David

I can't come out and tell him what he's holding.

Evan

Correct.

Cooper

I have this thing I need to return to you, but I am confused.

Johnson

Act, man. Act.

Ian

Put yourself in his shoes.

Evan

Guys.

Vince

But Mr. B., you have to feel it. You have to be it.

Evan

I know. Look, improv seems really scary to begin with, but in reality, you just do what you would do if you were in that scenario.

Cooper

In real life, I'd know what I was returning.

Evan

True. But, that's the point of the game. Good acting is hard. But you just have to feel it.

#6--ACT IT OUT!   –SONG

ALL

Act it out!
Show us some emotion! Show us some emotion!
Act it out!
Show us some commotion! Throw in some commotion!

Melody

Come on and
show it on your face

Johnson

Let us see the signs of grace
or of anguish or of fear or of pain--
show it HERE!

ALL

COME ON AND SHOW ON YOUR FACE!
SHOW US HOW YOU FEEL! COME ON MAKE IT REAL.

MAGNUS

WHAT WOULD A PERSON IN YOUR SHOES REALLY DO?????

ALL

ACT IT OUT!
SHOW US SOME EXPRESSION!
ABSOLUTE IMPRESSION!
ACT IT OUT!
MAKE IT LOOK REFRESHING,
NOT LIKE ALL THOSE EMPTY FACES ON THE WALL!

JADE

COME ON AND SHOW IT WITH YOUR WALK
AND YOUR MOVEMENT AND YOUR GAWK

TODD

USE YOUR ARMS, USE YOUR HANDS,
THINK OF HOW YOU STAND.
USE YOUR ARMS, USE YOUR HANDS,
THINK OF HOW YOU STAND.

KARA

WHAT WOULD A PERSON DO IF SHE WERE WALKING IN YOUR
SHOES??

BRYAN

COME ON AND SHOW IT WITH YOUR BOD
MAKE IT REAL!!!!!!

ALL

ACT IT OUT!
SHOW HOW YOU MOVE.

49

MAKE IT HARSH OR MAKE IT SMOOTH.
ACT IT OUT!
BUT ABOVE ALL MAKE IT REAL!!

MALES

COME ON AND SHOW US WITH YOUR VOICE,

FEMALES

LET US HEAR YOU'VE MADE A CHOICE IN CHARACTER
AND IN DELIVERY

ALL

WE WANT TO HEAR IT CLEAR,
AND WE WANT IT TO APPEAR
THAT YOU HAVE THOUGHT IT OUT!

IAN

JUST LIKE AN EAGLE SCOUT.
(TALENT SCOUT? RAINBOW TROUT?)

ALL

ACT IT OUT.
MAKE US WANT TO WATCH YOU.
MAKE US WANT TO CARE!
JUST ACT ...........IT...........OUT.

ACT I, SCENE 5

Margie

The garden seeds are sown. That's what makes a harvest. But there are always a few weeds to contend with.

The students begin to dissipate. Ruby Riley approaches.

Ruby

Magnus.

Magnus

Yes, grandma.

Ruby

How is my baby doing today?

Magnus

I'm okay. Just going to history.

Ruby

That's nice. Did you have a good drama class today?

Magnus

Sure. We got a lot done, and we got our assignment for the state contest.

Ruby

Oh, really. I'm sure you're all stoked about that.

Magnus

Yeah, this year it has to be an original musical about our lives. I hope I am able to be in it this year. I know there are limited spots.

Ruby

As always, dear. Say, who's that new young man walking out of the room?

Magnus

Oh, he's new. TJ something-or-other. He doesn't seem to like it much here.

Ruby

He'll learn. They all get the addiction.

Magnus

What?

Ruby

Nothing, Magnus. Everyone eventually finds a way to get
. . . hooked.

Magnus

Yep.

Ruby

One just has to figure out the bait.

Magnus

Grandma, are you okay?

Ruby

Yes, I'm fine. I just need to get back to my classroom. I am sure
that there are several students hanging from the ceiling by now.
You go on to class, dear.

Magnus

See you later.

Magnus leaves. Ruby turns her back to the audience.

Margie

Always thinking. Always plotting. Always secretly planning
revenge.

Diedre

Revenge. For what? What does . . . *(She has a revelation.)*
Oh! Yeah. I remember. She was . . .

Margie

Yeah.

#7--Ruby's Thoughts --MUSIC

Diedre

And her . . .

Margie

Yeah.

Diedre

And she never got over . . .

Margie

Yeah.

Diedre

Yeah.

Margie

Let's let her explain.

Ruby faces and talks directly to the audience.

Ruby

This is the part at which you get to hear what's going on inside an angry heart. Of course, I never voiced this out loud to anyone in my life. Those closest to me knew I was upset, and they knew why, but I was never one to share this turmoil with the world. I just waited for some way to use what I was feeling to get something done. You see, I am not in the wrong. I'm not the one who uses people for his own purposes. I don't fill people's minds with silly foolish ideas only to have them follow fanciful advice. My Cynthia, my darling girl fell for his foolish talk. She watched their little shows and actually sat in on a few of Evan Brighton's classes, if that's what you call them. And she got this horrid idea that she could move to New York to be an actress. Her, an actress. Oh, he never told her directly that she should quit her job, leave her child with me, and move to the big city, but he planted thoughts of grandeur in her head. And that's exactly what she did. She quit life, left Magnus with Grandma, and tried her hand at the stage. And I'm sure you can tell that it didn't work. She did nothing but wait tables, waiting for a big break, a BIG break, and the only thing she broke was my heart. She met some Frenchman who swept her off her feet, and all I got was a message that said, "Sorry, Mom. Have to try Europe with the man of my dreams. Take care of Magnus. I'll talk with you soon." And that was it. It's been over three years ago, and I haven't heard a single word. So, yes. I do have a legitimate concern with my superfluous colleague. And one way or another, I'll make sure he doesn't get away with destroying my family.

ACT I, SCENE 6

Diedre

Yeah.

Margie

Yeah.

Group enters.

Melody

Okay. We only have an hour to meet. We need to think of some good ideas.

Ruben

Shouldn't we wait until Mr. Brighton gets here.

Melody

Trust me. He'll appreciate the fact that we've been thinking of some ideas.

Vince

We need something that stands out. Lots of other schools will be doing the exact same thing.

Kara

That's right. We need something that's a bit different.

Crystal

But still has to be . . .

Several Students

believable.

Melody

Okay, what are the old plots. What do we know most people will write?

Olivia

Love.

Jade

So, we can't have love in the story?

Vince

We can. It just can't be the silly love stories everybody writes.

Magnus

What do you mean?

Vince

Girl pines after boy, goes crazy trying to get his attention.

Crystal

OR boy pines after girl, goes crazy trying. . .

Vince

Okay. Either one.

Evan shows up and watches undetected.

Trent

Or boy pines after boy . . .

Melody

I think we get it.

Kitt

How about a boy wanting a girl really badly and trying to get her.

Crystal

That's what we've been talking about, Kitt.

Logan

Did you take your medication today, Kitt?

Crystal

That's not nice, Logan.

Logan

But is it inappropriate?

Jade

He's so witty!

Olivia

(Aside to Jade) You have it bad for Logan, don't you?

Jade

Does it show?

Olivia

Like a cheap slip.

Melody

We're getting off-topic. I want to have some ideas for Bright.

Johnson

Can it have a variation of love?

Vince

I don't see why we can't include it. Does it need to be main focus?
If yes, okay. We just need to know.

Melody

No, let's make it a subplot, just to spice it up for people who need
that kind of thing in a play.

Ian

What kind of love? Unexpected love?

Kara

A secret affair?

Trent

Forbidden love?

Jade

Oooooo.

Johnson

What are we writing? A soap opera?

TJ

(From among the others) How about lost love?

Melody

TJ? I didn't know you were here.

TJ

Am I not welcome?

Vince

Of course, you're welcome.

Crystal

We just didn't expect you to be here. Welcome.

Quinton

I like lost love.

Logan

Get some new pants.

Crystal

Stop, Logan. Stop.

Logan

Have you seen his pants? You can see his religion.

Crystal

Do you have to be the commentator for life?

Logan

I am the only one bold enough to speak the truth?

Quinton

It's okay. I like my pants.

Logan

That's because . . .

Crystal

Logan!

Vince

Lost love is good.

Ruben

As a subplot?

Vince

Yes, we can work out the main plot with Bright. But if we had a subplot with . . .

Melody

Lost love.

Olivia

That might work.

Magnus

What kind of lost love?

Dakota

Someone breaks up.

Crystal

Too much like a soap.

Melody

Someone moves away? To a new place?

Jade

They can be followed?

Vince

Where could they never be followed?

Kitt

Death

Crystal

Death.

Melody

Death.

Vince

Someone loses his love to death.

Crystal

And it emotionally wrecks his private life.

Ruben

A girlfriend.

Jade

Yeah.

Vince

A fiancé.

Crystal

Yeah.

Evan

I can see haven't wasted any time.

Several Students

Mr. Brighton, Bright, etc.

Melody

We came up with some ideas for the contest piece.

Evan

Good. I actually heard a few of them.

Vince

You did?

Evan

Yes, I've been listening a few minutes.

Logan

Oh.

Evan

It's okay, Logan. Sometimes even truth is best left unsaid.

Olivia

Are you all right, Mr. Brighton?

Evan

I'm fine, Olivia.

Crystal

Well, did you like our ideas?

Evan

Yes, Crystal. I think they have a lot of potential. We'll flesh them out.

Everyone seems happy.

Evan

Of course, with one subplot down, we have to, at the very least, develop a main plot.

Ian

Therein lies the rub.

Evan

Good allusion, Ian.

Todd

I think I have writer's block.

Evan

It happens to the best of us. Luckily, we have a smart group here, and we can overcome anything.

Vince

I don't want to do perform a play just like everyone else's there. We won't stand out.

Evan

We won't do that then.

Kara

What would people NOT do?

Johnson

The better question may be to figure out what they WILL do.

Trent

And then through process of elimination . . .

Ian

Decide what we should do.

Evan

Thank you, my *trynamic* trio.

Dakota

Love is the subplot.

Crystal

Mr. Brighton, are you sure you're okay?

Evan

I'll be fine, Crystal.

Magnus

I'm sure we'll see parent problems.

Trent

Identity problems.

Dakota

Stories about bullies.

Melody

Stories about acceptance.

Ruben

Stories about "seizing the day."

Kara

Carpe Diem.

Logan

Gesundheit.

Kara

Gracias.

Johnson

Stories about finding meaning in the little things in life.

Todd

Stories about coping with death.

Olivia

Stories about revenge.

Logan

It's all BS.

Evan

Logan.

Logan

Sorry, Mr. Brighton. I mean it as "bull . . . stuff."

Ian walks to the back room to get a bottled water.

Evan

All those are valid stories real people face every day.

Logan

Yeah, but it's always the same thing with every teen drama. Ooh. Facing this, facing that. I want to be realer than real.

Vince

How about writing a musical about a group of teens writing a musical? (*Laughs*)

Everyone is silent.

Crystal

That's . . .

Melody

Good.

Ian re-enters.

Ian

(*Indifferently*) Mr. Brighton, Bryan's one tiny piece of fabric from full-on naked in the back room again.

Evan

(*Loud, but not yelling--almost unemotional*) Bryan, put your clothes back on.

Ian nonchalantly walks back to sit in his spot.

Vince

I already have some great ideas for some songs!

Evan

Good, Vince. Go with them. See what you can come up with.

Bryan re-enters wearing jeans, barefoot, and no shirt.

Bryan

But Mr. B. I like being naked. And honest: I'm trying on different costumes and stuff.

Evan

(*Nonchalantly*) Get naked at home. We don't need to deal with it here.

Bryan

Bummer. (*Sits, puts shirt on*) Where are my shoes? (*Looks*)

No one pays attention.

Josh walks in.

Josh

Sorry I'm late, Bright. I have a reason.

Evan

Tell me later, Josh.

Josh sits down, obviously upset about something.

Ruben

You okay, Josh?

Josh

Yeah. I will be.

Evan

I think that's a good idea.

Vince

We could write Josh a good lead part.

Josh

Guys. . .

Crystal

It's okay, Joshy. We know that's your part. We're not dumb.

Josh

But . . .

Vince

And I do fancy myself quite the songwriter. With your permission, Mr. Brighton, I'd love to get a few songs started for him and the rest.

Evan

Permission granted.

Olivia

So, are we writing a musical about writing a musical?

Evan

Is that what you guys want to do?

Several Students

Yeah. Sure. OK. We can try. Sounds good. That's the best idea.

Evan

TJ, you going to join us?

TJ

I suppose.

Evan

Excellent. OK. We need to divide up. We only have a little while before some of you need to go work and do other things. I need a few people to join Crystal and Melody on the plot structure. I need a few people to join Vince on songs. The rest of you can head on home if you need to. I have a booster club meeting in a few minutes.

Josh stands up and starts to go.

Evan

Josh, are you leaving?

Josh

I'm sorry, Mr. Brighton. I have to. I'll explain it you later.

As he leaves, Serena Joiner, Josh's mom enters for the booster meeting.

Serena

Josh.

Josh

Mom.

Serena

Are you leaving?

Josh

Yeah. I have to go. I'll talk to you later, OK?

Serena

OK.

She kisses him on the forehead, and he leaves.

Evan

Hello, Ms. Joiner.

Serena

How many times do I have to tell you, Mr. Brighton: please call me Serena.

Evan

But in front of the students . . .

Serena

Most of them know me as "Serena," too. That's my name.

Evan

All right.

Serena

What was up with Josh?

Evan

No clue. He was acting strange all afternoon.

Serena

I'll find out later I suppose. I'm early for the booster club meeting again I guess.

Evan

By just a little. Everyone is else is either going to be exactly on time or a bit late.

Caroline Adamson, town socialite and arts supporter, enters.

Caroline

Oh, Evan, sweetheart, how you are?

Evan

I'm good, Caroline.

Caroline

And Serena. How are you?

Serena

Good, Miss Caroline.

Caroline

And what are your sweet kids working so diligently, Evan?

Evan

We just got our assignment for the state theatre contest, and they're brainstorming and writing.

Caroline

Oh, is it that time again?

Evan

Yes, ma'am.

Serena

What's the assignment this year, Mr. Brighton?

Evan

An original musical about their lives.

Caroline

How precious. How precious. I can't wait to see how they do. I'll have to get my friends from the capital to meet me at the contest this year to show off our precious gems. Oh, and Serena, I know Josh will be the star. Your son is so talented. *(Looks at the students)* Where is he?

Serena

He had to leave.

Caroline

They are working so very hard.

Evan

Yeah. I need to let them work, so I am going to put up this sign to say we're going to move our booster club meeting to the library.

Caroline

Splendid idea, sweetheart. Do you want me to put up the sign?

Evan

Well, I haven't made it yet.

Caroline

Just give me a piece of paper, a marker, and some tape, and I'll be glad to take that task off your hands.

Evan

If you don't mind . . .

Caroline

Mind? I'd be delighted. And I'll go on down to the library to greet the rest of the club. I'm having some gourmet coffees and some scones catered in for the meeting. I'll leave a sign on the main entrance for the bistro to bring it all directly to the library. See you in a bit. Too-da-loo.

Evan

Thank you, Caroline.

Caroline leaves.

Serena

She always tires me out.

Evan

She means well.

Serena

How many disappointments started with that sentence?

Evan

Pardon me?

Serena

I'm sorry. I've just had a lot on my mind recently.

Evan

Join the club.

Serena

You, too?

Evan

After a while, you learn not to allow yourself to think. Or at least you fool yourself into thinking that's the case. (*Staring off*) You don't allow yourself to go some places.

Vince

Bright?

Evan

Yes, Vince?

Vince

How many songs do you think we need in the show?

Evan

Well, it's an hour show. That means no time for an intermission. You need a show opener that introduces the main character and as many minor characters as you can. You need a song that shows character conflict. You need a song in which the antagonist shows his need for actions against the hero. You need a big emotional group number past the half-way point. You need a song of revelation
and a song of peace at the end. That's six. That's probably too many for the sixty minutes, but if you get ideas or melodies for those,
you can always pick the strongest ones for the plot you end up with.

Vince

Six. Wow. I'll see what I can come up with.

Crystal

We already have two really good ideas.

Evan

That's great, guys.

Serena

(*Looking at Evan*) That's amazing.

Evan

What is?

Serena

How you just rattled that off like it's common knowledge.

Evan

It's my job, Ms. Joiner.

Serena

Ms. Joiner?

Evan

Serena.

Vince

Mr. Brighton. I'm going to have to call it quits for today.

Evan

That's fine, Vince. It sounds like you have a good start at the songs.

Vince

Yeah. And the rest of the group is going to stay and work for a few more minutes.

Evan

Okay.

Vince

Listen, I know you have to go to your booster club meeting and all, but could I ask you something first?

#8--Background--Worried Kids –Music

Evan

Sure. What is it, Vince?

Vince

Well, I don't know how to say this. Um. You know my brother.

Evan

Yes, I do. You know I taught him.

Vince

Yeah, know. Well, he's sort of getting into some things that I think are bad for him.

Evan

Bad for him?

Vince

You know, Mr. Brighton. Please don't make me spell it out.

Evan

Okay

Vince

He was in it a little in high school, but now in college, he's had a lot more access to it, and he's changing. I think he's about to drop out of school and everything.

Evan

Have you talked with your mom and dad about it?

Vince

Well, yeah. I've tried. Their minds are elsewhere. They are . . . well, not getting along too well.

Evan

I'm sorry, Vince.

Vince

It's OK. I've known it was coming for a long time, but the timing really sucks. I'm worried about Charlie. I can't be mom and dad for him.

Evan

You're not supposed to be. All you can be is Vince. Let him know you're worried about him and that you're there to help him, but don't nag him about it. That will only push him away. And with your parents having problems, he needs a brother.

Dakota

My parents are going through the same thing right now. I probably shouldn't tell anyone, but its driving me crazy. It's not fair.

Evan

No, it's not. And it's not your fault. Things happen a lot that all we can do it sit back and ask, "Where did that come from?"

Serena

Amen.

Vince

Amen.

Evan

I don't have any big answers for you. All I can say is just be yourself. Don't let it rob you of being who YOU are. Be there for your family and love them, but you can't let the situation destroy you. We're all going different places in our lives, and sad to say, none of us knows for certain where those places will actually be. But you're responsible for your places only. Love people, be there for them, but don't let yourself be drained of your potential and your energy. Believe me, life can really stink sometimes.

Serena

Amen.

All the Students

Amen.

#9--THERE ARE THINGS --SONG

EVAN

THERE ARE THINGS THAT YOU DON'T KNOW
ABOUT THIS WORLD.
THERE ARE PACTS AND TRENDS AND RULES
THAT CAN'T BE BROKEN.
THERE ARE DEALS TO GET THINGS DONE,
VIOLENCE LABELED FUN,
AND SACRIFICE IS YIELDED BY THOSE WHO DO NOT PAY.

WE'RE TOLD THE DREAM IS OUT THERE
FOR THE TAKING.
AND ALL WE HAVE TO DO IS JUST BELIEVE.
BUT WATCH THE THINGS YOU DO
AND THE PEOPLE YOU PURSUE
AND IF YOU OPEN UP YOUR EYES,
YOU'RE SURE TO SEE . . .

EVERY SILVER LINING HAS A CLOUD.
EVERY BRILLIANT RAINBOW HAS TO WAIT OUT THE RAIN.
EVERYTHING THAT'S GIVEN HAS A PRICE TO BE PAID.

AND YOU NEVER KNOW THE FEELING OF RELIEF
UNTIL YOU'VE FIRST KNOWN PAIN
OH! EVERY SILVER LINING HAS A CLOUD.

EVERY FLAME OF BRILLIANCE CAN BURN
LIKE THE SUN'S GLOW
EVERY HOPEFUL FEELING HAS TO FACE REALITY
BUT EVERYTHING YOU KNOW THAT CAN BE TRUE
--CAN BE TRUE,
IF YOU MAKE IT SO.

THERE ARE THINGS THAT SEEM
TO CHALLENGE ALL WE KNOW.
THERE ARE THOSE WHO SEEM TO LIVE ONLY TO FRUSTRATE
THERE ARE TIMES THAT WE DESPAIR

AND THEN SADLY FAIL TO CARE
THEN WE FIND THAT WE THEN ALIENATE OURSELVES

EVERY SILVER LINING HAS A CLOUD.
EVERY BRILLIANT RAINBOW HAS TO WAIT OUT THE RAIN.
EVERYTHING THAT'S GIVEN HAS A PRICE TO BE PAID.

AND YOU NEVER KNOW THE FEELING OF RELIEF
UNTIL YOU'VE FIRST KNOWN PAIN
OH! EVERY SILVER LINING HAS A CLOUD.

EVERY FLAME OF BRILLIANCE CAN BURN
LIKE THE SUN'S GLOW
EVERY HOPEFUL FEELING HAS TO FACE REALITY
BUT EVERYTHING YOU KNOW THAT CAN BE TRUE
--CAN BE TRUE,
IF YOU MAKE IT SO.

ACT I, SCENE 7

Diedre

I feel like I'm going to cry.

Margie

Here. (*Hands her a cleaning cloth, with which Diedre blows her nose.*) It's okay. You know the old saying about things getting worse before they get better.

Diedre

And I missed this.

Margie

You've been gone. Things happen. (*Pauses.*) But good things happen, too.

Evan is sitting at his desk working on his laptop. Vince, Crystal, Kara, Ruben, Melody, Olivia, and Josh enter.

Melody

Mr. Brighton!

Kara

Mr. Brighton.

Crystal

Mr. B!

Vince

We're finished!

Evan

With . . .?

Vince

The whole thing!

Crystal

The whole shebang.

Evan

All of it?

Vince

Yes, sir!

Olivia

Every word. Every line. Every jot. Every tittle.

Josh

(*Entering*) Every note.

Vince hands the script to Evan.

Evan

I'm very impressed, guys. You finished much earlier than I thought you would.

Josh

We couldn't stop. Once you get started on something like that . . .

Evan

Oh, I know.

Mr. Sebowski bursts into the room.

Sebowski

Well, well, well, what truants we have! What classes are you supposed to be in?

Josh

Lunch.

Sebowski

Lunch?

Melody

Lunch.

Sebowski

And why are you in here bothering Mr. Brighton.

Crystal

Bringing him our assignment for the state contest.

Sebowski

The state contest?

Logan

(*Entering*) Mr. B., there's a case of sudden deafness hitting the school.

Sebowski

What?

Logan

Pardon?

Sebowski

What did you say?

Logan

I'm sorry, Mr. Sebowski. I'm having troubles today. Not feeling well.

Evan

So, Logan. Is there an epidemic?

Sebowski

(*Frustrated and leaving*) Carry on.

Logan

Thank you.

Sebowski

Pardon.

Logan

Okay.

Sebowski leaves.

Evan

Logan, every time I start to scold you, I end up wanting to hug you.

Jade

Me, too.

Logan

I have that effect on people.

Vince

I don't want to hug you.

Logan

I have that effect on people, too.

Melody

Call it chemistry.

Quinton enters.

Logan

Sure smells like it.

Evan

Logan.

Logan

Hug me.

Evan

Lost the feeling.

Quinton

What's up, guys?

Logan starts to answer.

Evan

Logan.

Josh

Nothing much, Quinton.

Ian, Trent, and Johnson enter.

Ian

Play finished?

Vince

Yes.

Johnson

Where is it?

Trent

I want to see it.

Olivia

Bright has it now.

Evan

I need to read it first, guys.

Johnson

No problem, Mr. B. (*to Vince*) Is it good?

Vince

Better than.

Johnson

Sweet.

Trent

As "butta"

Ian

Part for me?

Vince

Most likely.

Melody

Of course.

Johnson

Part for me?

Josh

Most likely.

Quinton

Part for me?

Evan

Logan!

Logan growls in frustration.

Quinton

What?

Melody

(*To Quinton*) What?

Quinton

Is there a part for me?

Melody

We'll see.

Quinton

I'll bet there's a part for Josh.

Melody

Well, duh.

Ian pulls Trent aside for a conversation.

Ian

Hey. Quinton bothers me as much as the next guy, but they're pretty tough on him. Am I missing something?

Trent

It's all background, before you got into theatre.

Ian

Okay.

Trent

Quinton's just plain horrible, embarrassingly horrible on stage.

Ian

But . . .

Trent

And . . . Bright cast him and gave him a chance in a major show.
It was a disaster, the worst acting you that could possibly imagine.

Ian

But . . .

Trent

But . . . that wasn't the real problem.

Ian

Okay.

Trent

Quinton then starting trying out for everything, every production
and event over and over. Over and over! I mean over and over,
and he was so rude to Bright because he wasn't cast.

Ian

Ah.

Trent

Bright never cast him again. He couldn't. He tried that one time, but you know.

Ian

I see. He did try once I suppose.

Trent

Just because you want to do something doesn't mean that people have to let you do it with them. Do you know of one football coach, even one, who would allow someone to force him to put a bad player his team—one at all?

Ian

That's a good point.

Trent

Everyone's just tired of Quinton's attitude since he's been so mean about it, especially to Mr. Bright.

Magnus and Ruby enter.

Ruby

(With a fake smile) Afternoon, all. Wow, Mr. Brighton. We might as well rename your room the cafeteria.

Evan

It seems that way today.

Magnus

(Genuinely excited) So, did you guys finish the play?

Vince

Sure did.

Magnus

Great! Is there a part for me?

Logan

Here we go again.

Olivia

It's very likely.

Quinton

But . . .

Melody

Shhh. Shh. Quiet now. It's been a long day.

Ruby

Congratulations, students. Writing a complete musical is quite a task.

Magnus

What's it called?

Ian

Oh, I didn't ask!

Evan looks at the cover page.

Vince

"Tumble"

Evan

"Tumble"

Trent

Where'd you get "Tumble"?

Vince

Read it. It makes sense.

Olivia

Things happen. People tumble. Life recovers.

Vince

Shhh. Let them read it.

Olivia

Sorry, Tennessee Williams!

Vince

No problem, Blanche Dubois. In any case, my focus was the music.

Evan

Whoever did what, I'm very proud of you all. I look forward to reading it and seeing what we can do. Now, it's all of your jobs to make good grades and stay out of trouble so that we can perform and compete in a few months.

Ruby

Yes, be good. We wouldn't want your contest disrupted over something unfortunate.

TJ enters, carrying a backpack.

TJ

May I come in?

Evan

Certainly.

Josh

Get in here, kid.

Crystal

This is your home, too, TJ.

He puts his backpack near the wall--downstage on the actual stage--and takes a seat. During the course of the next several seconds, Ruby works her way to his backpack and--visibly to the audience--slips and sheet of paper in the outer pocket.

Vince

In fact, TJ, if Mr. B. approves, there may even be a part of a new student in the production.

Logan

Quinton, don't even.

TJ

Really? I don't know. I don't really know if I could even do something like that.

Vince

Sure, you could.

Olivia

I have a feeling you are capable of a lot more than you realize.

Ruben

The encouragement in here is infectious.

Quinton

Well, I think . . .

Melody

Shh. Shhh. Peace, love, and understanding.

Quinton

Are you people insane?

Logan

Pot. Kettle.

Evan

Logan.

Josh

We'll figure something out, TJ. I have some ideas. It's a really good script. I think we have a great chance this year. If some things work out . . . (*drifts*)

Melody

What things?

Josh

Nothing.

Crystal

What's wrong, Josh? For the past three weeks, you've been . . .

Josh

Nothing's wrong. I have to go. The play will go well; we'll win. (*Exits.*)

Olivia

Mr. Brighton, what's wrong with him?

Evan

I don't know, Olivia. I've been trying to figure it out myself.

Vince

But he IS right. We're going to do well this year, Bright. We're going places! This play has a lot of potential. I'm very excited.

Evan

I can tell. I am, too.

Crystal

There's no doubt that something big's about to happen.

Ruby

(Finished with her task, smiling) Indeed.

ACT I, Scene 8

A desk at which Mr. Stone, the high school principal, sits. Evan enters.

Evan

You wanted to see me?

Stone

Come on in, Evan. I have something to share with you.

Evan

Is something wrong?

Stone

Well, I think so. You know, as principal, I have to deal with many things, including many things I really don't like dealing with.

Evan

What's happened?

Stone

This. (*Hands Evan a sheet of paper. Evan reads it.*)

Evan

Wow.

Stone

We don't know who wrote it. But as you can see, the allegations are pretty strong. It involves several students, all of whom are in your program: Vince Forrester, T.J. Keller, Crystal Norris, Logan Ballard, Ruben Dillon, Melody Hoffman, and Olivia Carmichael.

Evan

Do you believe this?

Stone

Evan, I don't know what to believe. It's my job to figure that out. It does seem very suspect.

Ian

Of course.

Johnson

Magnus.

60

Vince

Evan

These are the cream of the crop, the best this school has to offer.

Stone

I know that.

Evan

They're outspoken and visible, but they are not dishonest. They don't have to cheat. Where was this found?

Stone

This particular note was left on my desk. After reading it, we brought in T.J. and searched his backpack. It was there that we found the history exam with all the answers and with evidence that suggested markings consistent with someone memorizing answers.

Evan

What did T.J. say about this discovery?

Sebowski

(*Entering*) He denied it, of course.

Stone

Mr. Sebowski, please.

Evan

Of course, he did. Wouldn't you if someone accused you of something out of the blue?

Sebowski

Well, if there were evidence right in my briefcase to disprove my protestations?

Evan

Make sure never to leave your briefcase unlocked, Mr. Sebowski. You never know what may accidently show up.

Sebowski

Convenient speculation, Mr. Brighton.

Stone

Gentlemen.

Sebowski

This is your total core of talent, Mr. Brighton. The kingdom crumbles.

Stone

Mr. Sebowski, that's enough. That is inappropriate on many levels.

Evan

Mr. Stone, I know anything is possible, but I would bet my reputation
that something's wrong here. I don't believe for a minute that those students cheated. They don't NEED to.

Sebowski

Maybe that is why their grades have been so high.

Stone

Mr. Sebowski, I think it's time you find somewhere to go for a little while.

Evan

Mr. Stone. Look at their total record. Look at their grades for years. This doesn't make sense.

Stone

Mr. Brighton, I'm not accusing. I'm investigating. I am trying to figure out what's going on.

Evan

It doesn't make sense.

Stone

I agree.

Sebowski

I don't.

Stone

Mr. Sebowski, good-bye.

Sebowski unwillingly leaves.

Evan

He's supposed to be a counselor, not a prosecutor.

Stone

Ignore him. Evan, I wanted to let you know what's happening. I have
to be honest with you: this doesn't sit well with me. Something's not
right here.

Evan

No.

Stone

This supposed exam has not even been given yet. I talked with
Mr. Mays, and he is planning on using that test right before his
semester final. It's based on what he's currently teaching.

Evan

Are you thinking what I think you're thinking?

Stone

I think so. Do you think I'm thinking about having Mr. Mays
surprise test these kids to prove they know this information?

Evan

And to show they would have no need to cheat?

Stone

Very possibly. BUT, we also have to figure out why the note was
on my desk and why the test was in T.J.'s backpack.

Evan

To come full-circle to our beloved counselor's statements, it's
all convenient.

Stone

Let's first see what these kids know. Then, we'll see where this "evidence" came from.

Diedre

So? What happened?

Margie

They called them in that very afternoon and Mr. Mays gave them an essay test on everything they had been learning. Needless to say, they were caught off-guard.

Diedre

But?

Margie

Yes, they all passed with flying colors. But there was still the issue of how this happened.

Diedre

But?

Margie

But . . . they never knew what happened. After they aced the exams, Mr. Brighton spent the entire afternoon working with Mr. Stone and battling Mr. Sebowski in the process for finding out where the note and the cheat sheet came from. There was no way to trace either one, but Mr. Stone acknowledged that anything can be slipped into anyone's bag.

The students are in Mr. Brighton's room. He returns.

Evan

It's over.

Vince

So???

Evan

There's no proof, and you all passed the exam.

They all breathe a sigh of relief, saying things like "Yes," "They should have known," "I'm so glad that's over," etc.

Evan

But it happened for some reason.

Olivia

What do you mean?

Evan

This didn't just happen. Someone planned this out and had a bigger goal.

Melody

Of stopping us?

Josh

Of destroying us.

Ruben

Of destroying us?

Evan

Yes.

Crystal

I can understand someone from another school feeling threatened by the competition. But here? Why?

Logan

Someone here is threatened.

Evan

(*Sitting*) Yes.

Vince

Bright, are you okay?

Evan

Yes, I'm just tired, Vince.

Melody

We may never know what happened.

Evan

Probably not, but you can rest assured it's not over.

#10--Background--It's Not Over Yet

Ruben

I'm confused.

Olivia

We all are.

TJ

Mr. Brighton.

Evan

Yes, TJ?

TJ

Thank you for standing up for me, for us.

Evan

You're welcome, TJ. It was the right thing to do. I'll stand up for you guys whenever I can and when I know something is fishy.

TJ

It could have gone bad. Thank you.

Vince

Yeah, thanks, Mr. B.

Josh

Bright, are you okay. You look bad.

Evan

I'm just worn out, Josh. I need to go home.

Josh

We need to let you then. Come on, guys, let's get out of here so Mr. B. can get his stuff together and go home.

The students get their belongings together and all say bye to Evan, some hugging him.

Vince

Take care, Mr. B. We've got a lot of work to do.

Evan

I know, Vince. Thanks.

Melody

Sleep!

Evan

Okay.

They start to leave. Josh is the last out the door.

Josh

There's a lot more going on than we all know. We can get through it, though. I've watched you for a long time now. You can do this. You've done it before.

Evan

Thanks, Josh.

Josh

Love ya.

Evan

Same here, kid.

Josh leaves.

Evan gets his belongings together, stands, looks around. During the course of this song, he leaves his room, shuts the doors, and continues to sing as he walks down the hall.

#11--JOURNEY TO SOMEWHERE --SONG

EVAN

WHEN I THINK OF WHAT COULD HAVE BEEN
ALL THE CHOICES I COULD HAVE MADE
ALL THE PATHS ON WHICH I COULD HAVE STAYED
ON MY JOURNEY TO SOMEWHERE.

WHEN I THINK OF WHAT MIGHT HAVE BEEN
ALL THE PEOPLE I NEVER MET
ALL THE ODDS OF WHICH I NEVER BET
ON MY JOURNEY TO SOMEWHERE, TO SOMEWHERE ELSE

THEN I WONDER, I WONDER WHY I AM HERE
NURSING NUMEROUS DOUBTS AND FEARS
DOING MY BEST TO SEE THE RAINBOW
THROUGH THE PRISM OF MY TEARS?

OH, I WONDER, I WONDER HOW I COULD BE
A PERSON OF INTEGRITY
WHO CAN HIDE HIS INSECURITIES
WITH SMILES AND THOUGHTS OF VICTORIES?

OH YES, I WONDER
HOW EFFECTIVE I REALLY AM
WITH THESE THOUGHTS THAT OFTEN SEEM
TO DAMN ME WHERE I STAND,

Serena, unseen by Evan, shows up, is surprised to see Evan leaving, and secretly watches as he sings and eventually leaves.

WHEN I THINK OF WHAT COULD HAVE BEEN
ALL THE ERRORS I COULD HAVE MADE
ALL THE PATHS ON WHICH I COULD HAVE STAYED
ON MY JOURNEY TO SOMEWHERE ELSE.

WHEN I THINK OF WHAT MIGHT HAVE BEEN
ALL THE TROUBLES I COULD HAVE MET
ALL THE PAINS FROM WHICH I COULD HAVE HAVE BET
ON MY JOURNEY TO SOMEWHERE,
TO SOMEWHERE WRONG.

THEN I KNOW,
I KNOW WHY I AM HERE
THOUGH I STILL HAVE MANY DOUBTS AND FEARS
I WILL STILL DO MY BEST TO SEE THE RAINBOW
THROUGH THE PRISM OF MY TEARS?

OH, I KNOW, I KNOW
HOW IMPORTANT IT IS TO BE A PERSON OF INTEGRITY
ON MY WAY HERE.
IF FOR JUST ONE SOUL.

Evan leaves. Serena sings the following section:

SERENA

THEN I KNOW, I KNOW WHY I AM HERE
THOUGH I STILL HAVE MANY DOUBTS AND FEARS
I WILL STILL DO MY BEST TO SEE THE RAINBOW
THROUGH THE PRISM OF MY TEARS?

OH, I KNOW, I KNOW HOW IMPORTANT IT IS
TO BE A PERSON OF INTEGRITY
ON MY WAY HERE.
IF FOR JUST ONE SOUL.

She looks sad, leaves the way she came in.

ACT I, Scene 9

Ruby enters and begins to look at all the bulletin boards and newspaper clippings dealing with the theatre group.

Ruby

(*To herself*) He's loved. He's adored. They hang on his every word: the kids, the administration, the newspaper, even the mayor. The kids used to come to me with their problems, but now it's Bright, Bright, Bright. Whatever I have to do, whatever . . .

#12--STOP HIM --SONG

She sings.

RUBY

A DAUGHTER IN NEW YORK OR PARIS WHO WON'T GIVE UP A DREAM
THAT'S FOOLISH AND QUITE USELESS AND TO BE A BIT OBSCENE.
AND WHOM CAN I THANK FOR THIS FOOLISH TURN OF FATE?

THE MAN THE CROWDS ADORE AND WHOM THEY THINK IS GREAT.

NOW EVERYWHERE I LOOK, I SEE HIS HANDIWORK
ON THE POSTERS, IN NEWSPAPERS, HIS CONSTANT PRESENCE
LURKS. HE'S LURING GENERATIONS TO FOLLOW IN HIS TRACKS.

ON THE POSTERS, IN NEWSPAPERS, HIS CONSTANT PRESENCE
LURKS. HE'S LURING GENERATIONS TO FOLLOW IN HIS TRACKS.
IT'S A BURDEN TO THE ONLY ONE WHO SEEMS TO KNOW THE FACTS.

IT'S UP TO ME. I HAVE TO STOP HIM.
THE PLAN IS UNDERWAY!
WHEN IT'S DONE, THE WORLD WILL DROP HIM. THERE WILL BE NO
SHADES OF GRAY.

IF I HAVE TO TELL THE BIGGEST LIE THE WORLD HAS EVER SEEN,
I'LL FEEL LIKE I AM JUSTIFIED IN BEING SLIGHTLY MEAN.

IT'S UP TO ME. I HAVE TO STOP HIM. HE'S SPREADING SEEDS OF
HOPE.

IT'S MY GOAL TO TRY AND CHOP HIM BEFORE HE LEADS A GROUP OF
DOPES

DOWN A PATH OF BIG IDEALS WHERE THEY FOLLOW FOOLISH
DREAMS
BY DOING WHAT THEY FEEL
AND CHOOSING PATHS EXTREME.

I HAVE TO STOP HIM.

I HAVE TO STOP HIM. I'M GONNA STOP HIM.

BEFORE HE LEADS SOMEONE ELSE INTO THEIR DREAM.

ACT I, Scene 10

Margie

Are you okay?

Diedre

I'm fine. Just watching.

Margie

I warned you things were different since you left.

Diedre

When it rains, it pours, doesn't it?

Margie

Wait until the storm.

Diedre

I don't know if I can watch.

Margie

If it helps, a few really good things happened first.

Diedre

Like?

Margie

"Tumble"

Diedre

Pardon?

Margie

"Tumble," the musical they wrote?

Diedre

Oh, really?

Margie

Yeah. And it well on its way.

Melody

(*Entering*) Sorry I'm late. I had to get an oil change, or my dad was going to never shut up about it.

Olivia

No problem. We're not to your part yet.

Vince

(*To the actors in rehearsal*) Okay, guys, Let's start with scene four.

Crystal

Okay.

Josh

You ready?

Vince

Yep.

Josh

(*Acting*) Where does this leave everything?

Crystal

Oh, Robert . . .

Josh

Things happen. I mean every promise I make. But life throws things at you sometimes. You can be dedicated and passionate and sincere and still get broadsided. It's not enough to be successful. Plenty of people are successful. People need to see integrity.

Crystal

Don't beat yourself up.

Josh

I'm not beating myself up. I'm being honest, maybe for the first time in my life.

Crystal

Oh, Robert.

#13--I TUMBLE ON THE ROAD   --SONG

JOSH

I HAVE ALWAYS TRIED TO BE THE ONE TO LEAN ON
I HAVE ALWAYS TRIED TO BE THE ONE TO ALWAYS GET
THINGS DONE I'VE ALWAYS HAD MY FOCUS
ON THE BULL'S EYE OF SUCCESS
AND I'VE OFTEN HAD THE ACCOLADES OF VICTORY

BUT NOW I'VE SEEN SUCCESS ALONE IS WORTHLESS
WITHOUT THE THINGS THAT MATTER MOST IN LIFE
I FIGHT A WINNING BATTLE, BUT I FEAR A LOSING WAR
AND I'M TIRED OF ALL THE AGONY AND STRIFE

I TUMBLE ON THE ROAD,
BUT I SEE THE BETTER GOAL
IT'S NOT WHAT I ACHIEVE.
IT'S WHAT IT'S MADE OF ME
I TUMBLE AND I STUMBLE
BUT I WOULDN'T CHANGE A THING

IT'S NOT WHAT I ACHIEVE.
IT'S WHAT IT'S MADE OF ME

I TUMBLE AND I STUMBLE
BUT I WOULDN'T CHANGE A THING
I'M PROUD OF THE JOURNEY
I'M HAPPY WITH THE VICTORY
BUT I'M HAPPIER BY FAR
WITH THE PERSON THIS JOURNEY'S MADE OF ME.

I have to go.

Vince

What?

Josh.

I have to go.

Crystal

Are you okay?

Josh

Yeah. Hold on. (*He leaves.*)

Evan enters right after Josh leaves.

Evan

I just passed Josh in the hall. Is he okay?

Crystal

I don't know. He just left.

Vince

Right in the middle of the song.

Evan

Maybe I should go check on him.

Melody

He's been getting weirder by the day.

Quinton enters.

Josh

BINGO.

Evan

Logan.

Quinton

Hello, everyone. Any parts open?

Vince

Not yet, Quinton.

Josh, visibly upset, enters.

Josh

Mr. Brighton, I need to talk with you.

Evan

Certainly. Do we need to take a walk?

Josh

Yes, sir. (*Pauses.*) No. No, sir.

Evan

Okay (*confused*)

Josh

I need to say this in front of everyone. I owe this to the whole team.

Crystal

What's wrong, Josh.

Josh

I've put this off, hoping I wouldn't have to do this, but (*Pauses*) I have to quit theatre.

Vince

What?!

Everyone echoes disbelief.

Logan

Is this a joke?

Quinton

Is there a part now?

Everyone

NO.

Evan

Josh, what's going on?

Josh

Mr. B, you know I love this. This is my passion.

Evan

Josh, what's going on?

Melody

Spit it out.

Josh

I'm going to be a father.

Everyone looks at each other and responds in shock.

Evan

A father.

Josh

Yeah. You know me. Always, well, you know. Eventually it was going to happen.

Vince

Are you sure?

Josh

That's what I'm told.

Evan

Josh, even if it is true . . .

Josh

Mr. Brighton, I know what you're going to say, and I have tried. Believe it, I have tried to find a way to do what I love and what I have to do, but it just won't work. I have to put what I have to do before what I want to do.

Evan

I understand. But you know that you can provide a lot more for a child if you have a college education.

Josh

I know. I still want to go, but I can't devote the time I need to you guys to make all this work. I'm sorry.

Evan

Okay. (*Pause*) Does your mom know?

Josh

I told her last night. I gotta go.

Evan

You know you are always welcome here, Josh. This is your family.

Josh

I know. Family's a powerful word.

He leaves.

Olivia

What now?

Vince

We're screwed.

Ruben

Can't someone else play Robert?

Vince

Not like Josh. I wrote it for him.

Quinton

Well . . .

Logan

Shut up.

Crystal

Can you change the role?

Vince

It's the main role, the whole thing is written around Robert.
I might as well write a new play, but we don't have time.

Evan

Well.

Ruben

Mr. B., what can we do?

Evan

I don't know, Ruben.

Olivia

We have to think of something.

Evan

We will.

TJ

Can I try?

Everyone looks at him.

Melody

What?

Vince

What did you say?

TJ

Can I try? The part? I know I'm not Josh, but if you need me, I can try.

The majority of the students look at Evan, waiting for his reaction.

Evan

If you want.

Vince

If you want.

Here. (*Hands him a script eagerly*) Scene 4.

Evan

Are you sure you want to try this, TJ? It's a big responsibility.
I don't say that to frighten you. I say it because it's true.
We're talking dedication.

TJ

I know. I want to try.

Evan

Okay.

Vince

Crystal, on stage please! Scene 4.

Crystal

Okay, okay.

Vince

And go!

TJ

(*Acting*) Where does this leave everything? (*He's good.
Everyone gradually starts smiling and glancing at Evan.*)

Crystal

Oh, Robert . . .

TJ

Things happen. I mean every promise I make. But life throws
things at you sometimes. You can be dedicated and passionate
and sincere and still get broadsided. It's not enough to be
successful. Plenty of people are successful. People need to
see integrity.

Crystal

Don't beat yourself up.

TJ

I'm not beating myself up. I'm being honest, maybe for the first time in my life.

Crystal

Oh, Robert.

#14--I TUMBLE ON THE ROAD. --SONG

TJ

I HAVE ALWAYS TRIED TO BE
THE ONE TO LEAN ON
I HAVE ALWAYS TRIED TO BE
THE ONE TO ALWAYS GET THINGS DONE
I'VE ALWAYS HAD MY FOCUS ON THE BULL'S EYE OF
SUCCESS AND I'VE OFTEN HAD THE ACCOLADES OF
VICTORY

BUT NOW I'VE SEEN SUCCESS ALONE IS WORTHLESS
WITHOUT THE THINGS THAT MATTER MOST IN LIFE
I FIGHT A WINNING BATTLE, BUT I FEAR A LOSING WAR
AND I'M TIRED OF ALL THE AGONY AND STRIFE

I TUMBLE ON THE ROAD,
BUT I SEE THE BETTER GOAL
IT'S NOT WHAT I ACHIEVE.
IT'S WHAT IT'S MADE OF ME
I TUMBLE AND I STUMBLE
BUT I WOULDN'T CHANGE A THING
I'M PROUD OF THE JOURNEY
I'M HAPPY WITH THE VICTORY
BUT I'M HAPPIER BY FAR
WITH THE PERSON THIS JOURNEY'S MADE OF ME.

How's that?

Evan

(With a smile of shock) Promising.

All the students begin showing excitement, running up to TJ, hugging and high-fiving him.

Evan

(Soliloquy) Promising. We don't know what's coming, but we have enough to survive. No, not to survive, to do well. That's what life's about though, isn't it?

#15--THE SWEET SURPRISE --SONG

SERENA

COULD YOU BE THE ONE
THAT I'VE BEEN LOOKING FOR?
COULD YOU BE AN ANSWER TO MY PRAYERS?
COULD THE QUITE UNLIKELY BECOME PROBABLE AT ONCE
BY TRUSTING I HAVE FOUND SOMEONE WHO CARES?

JOSH

COULD I BE THE REASON FOR MY PROBLEMS?
COULD IT BE I'M CHOOSING WAYS TO FAIL?
BUT CHANGING COURSE WOULD BE
AN ACKNOWLEDGEMENT OF FAULT
AND I REALLY CAN'T AFFORD TO FACE THE GAIL.

MELODY

COULD THE BLIND REFUSE TO SEE?

VINCE

COULD VISION CLEARLY BE

LOGAN

AVAILABLE AND FREE BUT WITHOUT THE GUARANTEE

OLIVIA

THAT THE VIEW WOULD BE WHAT THEY'D WANT TO SEE

IAN

COULD WE OPEN UP OUR EYES

TRENT

TO THE TRUTH THAT WE DISGUISE

JOHNSON

SO WE DON'T HAVE TO DESPISE

QUINTON

THE WORLD THAT WE SURMISE

RUBEN

FOR OUR THOUGHTS CAN THEN GIVE RISE

MAGNUS

TO THE LIFE THAT HOPE DEFIES

TO THE LIFE THAT HOPE DEFIES

KARA

AND THEN THERE WILL ARISE

DAKOTA

THE SWEET SURPRISE.

ALL

THE SWEET SURPRISE

TJ

THAT UNEXPECTED GLIMMER
YOU NEVER WOULD HAVE DREAMED
WOULD COME YOUR WAY

ALL

THAT SWEET SURPRISE

SERENA

THAT ACCIDENT OF HAPPINESS THAT MAKES YOU KNOW
TOMORROW WILL BE BETTER THAN TODAY

JOSH

THAT SWEET SURPRISE

EVAN

THAT LEADS YOU TO BELIEVE THAT
THOUGH EVERYTHING IS STACKED AGAINST YOU

EVAN AND SERENA

STILL YOU CAN REPRISE

EVAN, SERENA, JOSH, AND TJ

THAT SIMPLE SONG WITHIN YOUR HEART

VINCE

THAT DROP OF HOPE ALIVE

EVAN

THAT DROP OF HOPE ALIVE

EVAN

THE SWEET SURPRISE.

IAN, TRENT, JOHNSON

AND WHEN IT SEEMS THAT ALL YOUR HOPE IS GONE
AND YOU HAVEN'T STRENGTH TO CARRY ON

VINCE, CRYSTAL, OLIVIA

WAITING JUST OUTSIDE THE OPENING DOOR

ALL

IS

CRYSTAL

THE SWEET SURPRISE

ALL

THAT UNEXPECTED GLIMMER
THAT YOU NEVER WOULD HAVE DREAMED
WOULD COME YOUR WAY
THAT SWEET SURPRISE
THE ACCIDENT OF HAPPINESS
THAT MAKES YOU KNOW
TOMORROW WILL BE BETTER THAN TODAY
THAT SWEET SURPRISE

THAT LEADS YOU TO BELIEVE
THAT THOUGH EVERYTHING IS STACKED AGAINST YOU,
STILL YOU CAN REPRISE
THAT SIMPLE SONG WITHIN YOUR HEART THAT DROP OF
HOPE ALIVE
THE SWEET SURPRISE

THE SWEET SURPRISE!

Lights down on main cast.

#16--Background--Ending of Act I--Music

Margie

Diedre. Are you breathing?

Diedre

Yes. I'm breathing. I'm okay. It's like watching a soap opera but with people I know and care about.

Margie

I've been here every day. I know. I tell you what. I have to finish this story, but before I do, why don't you take a break, get a drink or a bite to eat.

Diedre

I may take a ten-minute nap.

Margie

Do what you need to do, darling. Let's take a short break, and since we're in the theatre, we can call it . . .

Diedre

(*Looks at audience*) Intermission.

Lights Out.

END of ACT I

ACT 2
Act 2, Scene 1

#18--Background--The Refocus --MUSIC

Margie

Okay. I almost fell asleep. I have to be honest: this isn't the easiest job in the world. But, it's a lot more interesting than people realize.

Diedre enters downstage right.

Well, did you get everything taken care of?

Diedre

I tried. You know, I turn off my cell for a few minutes, and everyone starts calling.

Margie

Uh-huh.

Diedre

Where were we?

Margie

If I remember, we had a few problems and a few rays of hope. Places!

Vince enters and sings. As he sings, Crystal, Logan, Melody, Olivia, and TJ enter.

#19--SWEET REPRISE –SONG

VINCE

THAT UNEXPECTED GLIMMER
THAT YOU NEVER WOULD HAVE DREAMED
WOULD COME YOUR WAY

THE ACCIDENT OF HAPPINESS
THAT MAKES YOU KNOW
TOMORROW WILL BE BETTER THAN TODAY

LOGAN

THAT LEADS YOU TO BELIEVE THAT
THOUGH EVERYTHING IS STACKED AGAINST YOU,

OLIVIA

STILL YOU CAN REPRISE

MELODY

THAT SIMPLE SONG WITHIN YOUR HEART

TJ

THAT DROP OF HOPE ALIVE

CRYSTAL

THE SWEET SURPRISE

#20--THE PART REPRISE –SONG

Most of the rest of the students appear on stage as the music transitions in the song "To Play the Part." As they all sing this song, they work on various theatre activities: scene work, set building, costume fitting, makeup application, etc.

FEMALES

WITH CHOICES TO BE MADE
WE DEFINE THE ROLES THAT MUST BE PLAYED
WE MAY BE ON A STAGE OR JUST A STAGE WITHIN OUR LIVES

MALES

BUT IF THE TRUTH BE TOLD
WE CREATE THE ROLES THAT DO UNFOLD
AND WITHIN THIS PART, WE FIND THE COURAGE TO SURVIVE!

ALL STUDENTS

WE PLAY . . .
OH, WE PLAY THE PART!
WHAT AN AMAZING TASK WE HAVE!
TO NOT ONLY ACT BUT ACT
WITH STRENGTH OF COURAGE AND OF TRUTH.

LOGAN

WE CHOOSE TO REMEMBER WHO WE ARE!

ALL STUDENTS

AND NEVER SACRIFICE OUR SOULS TO WHOM WE WISH TO BE!!

Music fades.

Vince

(Walks up to Melody) So, how's he doing today?

Melody

He's working on it.

Vince

What does that mean? You're scaring me.

Melody

He'll be just fine. He's not a Josh, but he'll just fine.

Vince

We have a few weeks yet. I have faith.

Melody

You hold on to that. (Leaves.)

Vince

(Nervous.) What's that supposed to mean? Melody!

Logan approaches Vince.

Logan

How's TJ doing with the new part?

Vince

Melody says he's doing great, so he's doing great.
Just great. (Leaves.)

Logan

OK

Jade

Approaching. Hello, Logan!

Logan

Hello, Jade. Gotta jet. See you at the fittings. (*Leaves.*)

Crystal enters.

Crystal

What's wrong?

Jade

Life.

Crystal

What?

Jade

Everybody's in such a mood. This isn't fun.

Crystal

It's not always about fun. There are days that are definitely not fun. But it takes those days to make us better.

Jade

Well, you need to tell everybody that then.

Crystal

OK. I will. EVERYBODY!!! Get out here. I need so see you on stage.

All the students enter in rounds, saying "What's wrong?" etc.

Crystal

It's nothing bad. It's just that we need to cheer up.

Vince

Oh.

Crystal

Yes, oh. Things may seem tough right now but we are
going to pull through this.

Melody

Crystal, darling, we are all under the stress of deadlines
and classes and bad moods and pulling this show together
and a lot of changes. Yes, things are tough, and we are feeling it.

Crystal

Melody, sweetheart, I know. We are all feeling it. I just don't want
us to forget who we are. This isn't about one of us; it's about all
of us. It's not just about winning; it's about knowing that what we're
doing makes us better. We will take this with us forever. We are
part of something amazing. And even when we are stressing out,
we can know . . .

#21--THE COMPANY-TEAM SONG --SONG

CRYSTAL

IT IS TIME.
OH, IT IS TIME.
IT IS TIME TO GET STARTED

TO FINISH WHAT WE'VE STARTED.
IT'S NOT THE ENDING.
IT'S JUST THE ENDING OF THE BEGINNING OF THIS TALE

Gradually, the students' attitudes start improving, and they get happier.

AND THE BEGINNING OF THE ENDING OF THE TALE--
IT'S NOT COMPLICATED.
NOT COMPLICATED AT ALL.

LOGAN

WHAT DOES THIS SOUND LIKE A FUNERAL
WHEN IT'S A PARTY?

LOGAN, TJ, VINCE, MAGNUS

WE'RE A TEAM, AND WE'RE GOING TO ACT LIKE ONE.
WE CAN ACT AND WE CAN SACRIFICE AND DO WHAT IT TAKES

MELODY, OLIVIA, JADE, CRYSTAL

WE'RE A TEAM, AND WE'RE GOING TO ACT LIKE ONE.
WE ARE MORE THAN OUR COMPONENTS, AND WE'RE DEALING WITH
HIGH STAKES.

LOGAN, TJ, VINCE, MAGNUS, MELODY, OLIVIA, JADE, CRYSTAL

AND PEOPLE DO NOT UNDERSTAND IT.
THEY ASSUME WE'RE JUST A GROUP OF DRAMA NERDS.
BUT ONCE THEY CLIMB ABOARD AND LAND IT.
THEN THEY SEE THAT WE'RE A TEAM WHO MASTERS EMOTIONS,
ACTIONS, THOUGHTS, AND WORDS!

During the following part of the song, Ruby enters with pen and paper, finds a place to write and, in view of the audience, begins, deliberately and with great thought, writing some sort of letter. However, she is unaware of the students, and they are unaware of her.

ALL STUDENTS

WE'RE A TEAM, AND WE'RE GOING TO ACT LIKE ONE.
WE'RE A TEAM, AND WE'RE GOING TO ACT LIKE ONE.
WE'RE A TEAM, AND WE'RE GOING TO ACT LIKE ONE.
WE'RE A TEAM, AND WE'RE GOING TO ACT LIKE ONE.
WE'RE A TEAM, AND WE'RE GOING TO ACT LIKE ONE.
WE'RE A TEAM, AND WE'RE GOING TO ACT LIKE ONE.
WE'RE A TEAM, AND WE'RE GOING TO ACT LIKE ONE.
WE'RE A TEAM, AND WE'RE GOING TO ACT LIKE ONE.
WE'RE A TEAM, AND WE'RE GOING TO ACT LIKE ONE.
WE'RE A TEAM, AND WE'RE GOING TO ACT LIKE ONE.
WE'RE A TEAM, AND WE'RE GOING TO ACT LIKE ONE.

WE'RE A TEAM, AND WE'RE GOING TO ACT LIKE ONE.
WE'RE A TEAM, AND WE'RE GOING TO ACT LIKE ONE.
WE'RE A TEAM, AND WE'RE GOING TO ACT LIKE ONE.
WE'RE A TEAM, AND WE'RE GOING TO ACT LIKE ONE.
WE'RE A TEAM, AND WE'RE GOING TO ACT LIKE ONE!!!

WE ARE A . . . COMPANY!
A PROFESSIONAL COMPANY.
WE TACKLE THE TASK, TO DO WHAT WE'RE ASKED
THEN DO ANY MORE TO BE TRIUMPHANT--WE
ARE A COMPANY
MORE THAN A GROUP JUST DOING ITS OWN THING.

WE ARE FOCUSED, WE ARE READY,
WE ARE LOYAL, WE ARE STEADY.
WE WILL DO WHAT IT TAKES TO BE REAL TO BE A COMPANY.

AND NOW IT'S TIME.
NOW IT'S TIME.
NOW IT'S TIME

Evan

(*from offstage*) Pizzas are here, guys!

ALL STUDENTS

FOR THE COMPANY
PARTY!

Song ends. All the students exit the stage.

Ruby

(*Folds her letter. Smiles.*) Let the party begin.

127

Act 2, Scene 2

Diedre

Wait. What did she just do?

Margie

You'll see.

Diedre

But she . . .

Margie

You'll see.

Jade sits downstage and eats something (apple, bag of potato chips, something crunchy and obvious.) She appears to be in deep, depressed thought.

Olivia walks by reading a script. She notices Jade.

Olivia

Jade. You okay?

Jade

Oh, hi, Olivia. Yeah, I'm fine.

Olivia

You don't sound like you're fine.

Jade

Eh.

Olivia

It's Logan, isn't it? Still can't get him to notice?

Jade

It's like he's blind. Maybe he's just not into me.

Olivia

Never talk that way. Men don't get the choice. "We" decide who we date. They're just there to find out who they get.

Jade

You really believe that?

Olivia

There's nothing to "believe." It's fact. Women decide. We focus on who we want and then we do what it takes to make them think that they are in control and want to choose us. That's one of the biggest secrets of humanity, Jade. That's where the real power is. And then the rest of the world pretty much is run on what we say and want.

Jade

You're serious? I had no idea. You mean if I want Logan, I can get him?

Olivia

If you want Logan, it's a done deal. He'll be yours. Just come with me. I can show you exactly what you need to do to make your domination complete.

Jade

(Gets up, smiling.) Okay. And here I was thinking that true love happened when a boy and a girl looked into each other's eyes and felt that mutual click.

Olivia

Jade, that click is the remote control on a Hollywood movie, made by men. You're about to learn the ways of the real world.

They leave.

Mr. Brighton walks in with a stack of books and places them on his desk. His back is to the door. Josh enters sheepishly.

Josh

Bright?

Evan

(Turning around, pleasantly surprised.)
Josh! How long have you been standing there?

Josh

I just got here.

Evan

How are you?

Josh

I'm okay. You got a sec?

Evan

Of course. Come on in.

Josh

Thanks.

Evan

So, what's up?

Josh

I don't know where to begin. I am so sorry about letting you down, quitting.

Evan

Josh, don't . . .

Josh

No, Bright. Let me finish. Please. I have to say this.

Evan

Okay.

Josh

I messed up really bad. I went out and got this girl pregnant, and Mr. B, I don't even know if I believe her. She's acting really funny about it all.

Evan

Well, if she's pregnant, Josh, she is dealing with a lot herself.

Josh

It's more than that. It's like it's not even real. I can't explain it. But, nevertheless, it's my responsibility, and I will take care of my responsibility. But it tears me up that I let all of you down. I don't know how this happened.

Evan

Josh, you KNOW how this happened.

Josh

Yeah, I know HOW it happened.

Evan

Even at that, Josh, you have quite the reputation for . . . well, living.

Josh

(Laughs.) No, I haven't exactly been the poster child for celibacy.

Evan

Not exactly.

Josh

I'm sorry, Mr. B. I know I let you down. That's all I can think of.

Evan

Well, Josh. I wish things had turned out differently, yes, but as far as letting me down, I don't see it that way. The fact that you're sitting
here right now says a lot. I'm proud of you for who you are.

Josh

(Hugs Evan.) And there's something else.

Evan

What?

Josh

I have to make a living for my kid. I have to do the right thing. I know I have to make money right now, and I gladly do that. But I can't think of anything for the long run. I just can't work flipping burgers until I'm seventy. I have to do something that I love so that I can pass that passion on. Does that make any sense?

Evan

Perfect sense.

Josh

I mean, I have to find something that I love to do and can make a living at even if it's not tomorrow. I have to have a goal, a passion.

Evan

I'm sure I know the answer to this question, but what do you really, really want to be? What can you imagine as the only possible thing you could ever enjoy?

#22—AN ACTOR –SONG

JOSH

I WANT TO BE AN ACTOR

Evan

(*Spoken*) I knew it.

JOSH

I WANT TO WALK RIGHT INTO VIEW TO BE ON STAGE
TO BE THE RAGE
OF THE COUNTRY AND THE WORLD

I WANT TO BE AN ACTOR
I DON'T REALLY CARE ABOUT THE FAME

BUT IF I TURN ON THE NEWS
OR SKIM THROUGH "THE VIEW"
AND HEAR MY NAME

Evan

(*Spoken*) Josh, you know that people don't understand it? Until they walk
on that stage, they never know.

(SINGS)

WHAT A NOBLE DREAM YOU HAVE TO BE AN ACTOR
YOU CAN USE WHAT YOU HAVE LEARNED AND LEARN WHAT
YOU HAVE USED
TO MAKE THE GIANT STEP . . .

JOSH

I WANT TO BE AN ACTOR
IF IT'S ON STAGE OR ON THE SCREEN
TO CAUSE LAUGHTER UNTIL TEARS
OR HELP THOUSANDS FACE THEIR FEARS
OR A PERSON WHO FEELS HOPELESS REACH A DREAM

EVAN

FROM THE TIME OF THE GREEKS
ACTORS ROSE TO SPEAK
AND THEY TALKED ABOUT THE WORLD THAT THEY CALLED
HOME
THROUGH THE AGES, THEY'VE REFLECTED
ALL THE TRUTHS THAT THEY'VE SUSPECTED
AND THEY'VE BEEN A STEADY BEACON AS WE'VE ROAMED

JOSH

THERE WAS SOPHOCLES, EURIPEDES, HEROIC TALES OF
HERCULES
THE ROMAN PLAYS OF HUMOR AND OF VICE

EVAN

PLAYS OF MYSTERY, MORALITY, EVERYMAN'S IDENTITY
TRAVELERS' TALES, THE PASSION OF THE CHRIST

JOSH

BURBAGE HAD HIS PLAYERS, MARLOWE WROTE IN LAYERS
SHAKESPEARE AND HIS KING'S MEN GOT THE FAVOR OF
THE CROWN

EVAN

WOMEN BROKE THE CEILING, MOLIERE SHOWED US
FEELING
AMERICA HAD PLAYERS VISIT EVERY WESTERN TOWN

JOSH

STANISLOVSKI TAUGHT THE METHOD

THEN BRECHT NEVER RESTED UNTIL HE FOUND A WAY TO
BREAK THAT PESKY FOURTH WALL

EVAN

STRASBERG AND ADLER, HAGEN AND MEISNER
OPENED UP THE DOORS TO THE ACTING BALL

JOSH

WITH HOFFMAN, CLIFT, DEAN, MONROE
NEWMAN, WOODWARD, AND BRANDO
SHEEN, KEITEL, AND LEMMON AND MACLAINE

EVAN

BEATTY, REDFORD, NICHOLSON
MINELLI EVEN GENE HACKMAN
DE NIRO AND PACINO AND MCSWAIN

JOSH

DUVALL AND PECK AND VOIGHT AND CAGE
TOMMY HANKS IS ALL THE RAGE
PITT AND CLOONEY, BERRY, KIDMAN
CRUISE AND FORD AND PENN

EVAN

FREEMAN, STREEP, DICAPRIO
NORTON, SMITH, AND RUSSELL CROWE
BALE AND DAMON, ROBERTS, GABLE
WINSLET AND EVEN CHRIS WALKEN

JOSH

DENCH, TRAVOLTA, TRACY, CAINE
JACKMAN, NEESON, GABLE, WAYNE
CONNERY, OLIVIER, BULLOCK, WILLIS, LEIGH

EVAN

EASTWOOD, LEDGER, BOGART, COOPER
WASHINGTON, MCKELLAN, HOPPER

THE POWER OF THE CRAFT IS SO STRONG—YOU MUST
AGREE

JOSH

I WANT TO BE AN ACTOR
I'M TIRED OF FAKING WHAT I WANT
PRETENDING, ACTING NONCHALLANT ABOUT IT ALL

EVAN

THERE'S NO WAY YOU CAN UNDERSTAND
UNTIL YOU WITH THOSE STAND HANDS
FEELING YOUR ADRENAL GLAND
PREPARE YOU FOR THAT HAPPY LAND
THERE ON THE STAGE WHERE YOU STAND

JOSH

I WANT TO BE AN ACTOR
ONCE YOU TASTE IT, YOU CAN'T LOSE IT

EVAN

AND THEN YOU CAN'T REFUSE IT

JOSH

IT'S A CALLING. IT'S A PASSION.

EVAN

IT'S A DREAM

JOSH

I CAN DO IT

EVAN

YOU CAN DO IT

JOSH

AND I CAN GET THROUGH IT

EVAN

INTEGRITY AND HONESTY

JOSH

TRANQUILITY, HUMILITY
I WANT TO BE

BOTH

AN ACTOR

Song ends.

Evan

You know, that's a long-range plan now. You have a baby to care for.

Josh

I know. But it is a possibility for my future. Don't you think?

Evan

Josh, very few people have the gift you do. It shouldn't be wasted. A lot of people don't understand what a profession theatre can be. It's not just playing. It's a noble profession that had served mankind since ancient times. If you feel it's your calling, don't let anyone stop you from pursuing it. Life's too short to let things . . .

Bright, you okay?

Evan

Yeah. Just thinking.

Josh

You know, Mr. B., the "life's too short" stuff applies to you, too.

Evan

Okay, Josh, let's not get too deep here. Come help me with some more books I need to move.

Josh

At your service, sir.

As Evan and Josh leave the stage, we see Mr. Stone at his desk working. Ruby enters, crying.

Ruby

Mr. Stone, may I talk with you?

Stone

Of course, Ms. Riley. (*He gets up to pull out her chair.*) What's the matter?

Ruby

Well, I feel silly about this, but I think it's my duty to share this vital information with you.

Stone

What is it?

Margie

And then she told him.

Diedre

(Anxious.) Told him what??

Margie

The following story should be acted out in pantomime as much as possible.

The whole story of Cynthia, her daughter, how she had been affected by all the plays here and the inspiration of Mr. Brighton, and how she had gone away to try to become an actress in New York. And she told him how she had fallen in love with a Frenchman and how she had moved to Paris, never to be heard from again and how she had had to raise Magnus all alone, without his mother's help. Then, she told him of something she said had just happened.

Diedre

What?

Margie

Something horrible. She said that just received a letter without return address, but postmarked from Paris. She said this letter was in her daughter's hand. She said her daughter claimed to safe from harm, but she could never return to the US and especially to her hometown, because the man she looked up to, who had inspired her, had violated that trust and had taken advantage of her, and that she had to leave so as not be near him--because of her fear.

Pantomime over.

Diedre

Mr. Brighton???

Margie

Mr. Brighton.

Diedre

You've got to be kidding.

Margie

No.

Diedre

Bright wouldn't hurt a fly.

Margie

I think that's what Mr. Stone thought, too, but he had to be cautious. You know how those things go.

Diedre

Wow.

Margie

So, as you can tell, things started spiraling all at once in our little wing of Legacy Road. Emotions are on the rise, too. When it rains, it pours.

Act 2, Scene 3

Actors enter the stage one-by-one to speak. When finished, they remain to sing on the next song.

Melody

I'm doing it. I'm assistant directing this show! Mr. B. asked me to be the official assistant director, and he is letting me make a lot of the decisions.

Ruben

I'm getting better. I'm doing the very best I can, and I'm getting better. Even Melody is giving me compliments.

Vince

I'm seeing music that I wrote on stage. I can't believe it. It's great. People like it, and they're singing it. I even hear them humming it going down the halls. Look out, Sir Andrew!

Crystal

It's all coming together. TJ's working out well. They whole thing's going great. I miss Josh, of course, but we can do this.

Logan

It's coming together better than I thought it would. We've managed to keep Quinton out of the show. I have to keep insisting. Mr. B.'s an ol' softie. Somebody has to help him be tough.

Jade

Things are going to work out exactly as planned. I have faith.

Olivia

Oh, yeah!

TJ

I'm going to do this. I can't believe it, but I'm going to do this. I had no idea when I walked in that door months ago, but I am glad it's working out this way. It feels right. That's all I can trust right now. It feels right.

Serena

I don't know what to say. My son's gotten himself into a fix, but he is being responsible and stepping up to the plate. I still volunteer quite a lot, but I have come to think that . . . no, I've come to believe that . . . well, I'm in love with Evan Brighton.

Evan

Things are going so well right now, that I'm scared to jinx them. I was really worried about Josh, but I have a feeling that will be okay. The rest of the kids have risen to the occasion and have put together a top-quality production. It's all going extremely well. I'm proud.

#24--I'VE NEVER SEEN A SKY SO BRIGHT –SONG

EVAN

I'VE NEVER SEEN THE SKY SO BRIGHT
I'VE NEVER SEEN THE SUN PUT OUT SUCH LIGHT
I'VE NEVER SEEN A DAY SO FULL OF PROMISE AND OF HOPE
I'VE NEVER SEEN A WORLD SO NEW
I'VE NEVER SEEN MY PROBLEMS BE SO FEW
I'VE NEVER SEEN SKY, I'VE NEVER SEEN A SKY SO BRIGHT.

MALES

COULD IT BE THE WORLD IS "SMILING" . . . TODAY?
COULD IT BE THE WEIGHTS SEEM WEAK AND FLOATING . . . AWAY?
COULD IT BE I UNDERSTAND THE DESTINY THAT IS AT HAND?

FEMALES

COULD IT BE I DON'T FEEL...GLOOM?
COULD IT BE THAT THERE'S . . . SOME . . . ROOM
FOR . . . HOPE??????

ALL

I'VE NEVER SEEN THE SKY SO BRIGHT
I'VE NEVER SEEN THE SUN PUT OUT SUCH LIGHT
I'VE NEVER SEEN A DAY SO FULL OF PROMISE AND OF HOPE
I'VE NEVER SEEN A WORLD SO NEW

I'VE NEVER SEEN MY PROBLEMS BE SO FEW
I'VE NEVER SEEN SKY, I'VE NEVER SEEN A SKY SO BRIGHT.

EVAN

COULD IT BE THAT LIFE SPRINGS NEW
WITH THE GLORY OF THE POSSIBILITIES OF
WHAT COULD BE
OR WHAT COULD BE
SO, I NEVER HAVE TO WONDER
ABOUT WHAT COULD . . .HAVE . . . BEEN?

ALL

I'VE NEVER SEEN THE SKY SO BRIGHT
I'VE NEVER SEEN THE SUN PUT OUT SUCH LIGHT
I'VE NEVER SEEN A DAY SO FULL OF PROMISE AND OF HOPE I'VE
NEVER SEEN A WORLD SO NEW
I'VE NEVER SEEN MY PROBLEMS BE SO FEW
I'VE NEVER SEEN SKY, I'VE NEVER SEEN A SKY SO BRIGHT.

SERENA

(BRIDGE)
IF I LIVED A MILLION YEARS OR MORE,

LOGAN

IF I FOUND THE SPOILS OF ANCIENT WARS,

CRYSTAL

IF I HAPPENED ON THE MYSTERIES OF ALL BEING AND OF TIME,

RUBEN

IF I LEARNED THE WISDOM OF THE SAGE,

OLIVIA

READ EVERY WORD ON EVERY PAGE,

VINCE, EVAN

I'D NEVER FIND THE PEACE I FEEL JUST WAKING UP TODAY.

ALL

(CHORUS)
I'VE NEVER SEEN THE SKY SO BRIGHT
I'VE NEVER SEEN THE SUN PUT OUT SUCH LIGHT
I'VE NEVER SEEN A DAY SO FULL OF PROMISE AND OF HOPE I'VE
NEVER SEEN A WORLD SO NEW
I'VE NEVER SEEN MY PROBLEMS BE SO FEW
I'VE NEVER SEEN SKY, I'VE NEVER SEEN A SKY SO BRIGHT.

Song ends.

Everyone walks off except a smiling Evan.

Mr. Stone and Ruby approach.

Stone

Mr. Brighton, may I speak with you a few minutes.

Evan

Sure. What's up?

Stone

We have a problem.

Evan

Are you okay, Ruby?

Ruby

No. I don't want to believe it, Evan. *She turns her back to him.*
(Grins.) I don't want to believe it can be true, but I have no
choice.

Evan

What are you talking about?

Stone

Here, Evan. This is the only way to explain it. (*He hands Evan the letter. Evan reads. Disbelief slowly starts to spread across his entire demeanor.*)

Ruby

I just don't want to believe it. But it's my Cynthia. This explains everything.

Stone

Ms. Riley, this letter was sent from suspect origins, as the officer said.

Evan

Officer?

Stone

Yes, Evan. You understand that I had to call the police and tell them everything that Ms. Riley shared with me. This is a very serious accusation, even if it can't be substantiated at this time.

Evan

It's VERY serious. It's also very untrue. I in no way did any of these things. I barely knew the lady.

Ruby cries.

Stone

I understand, Evan. Nonetheless, I need to ask you to come to my office a few minutes to meet with the officer.

Evan

Is my job in jeopardy?

Stone

(Quietly, even though Ruby tries to listen over her own tears.)
No. Not now. This is very little proof of anything. We just
need to cover everything and keep it on the up and up. Let's
go to my office.

Evan rises, weak, to accompany Mr. Stone.

Stone

Let me stress to you both that I do not want this discussed
with anyone at this time. It is off limits to anyone. It's enough
that we have one additional person who, thanks to thin walls,
knows.

Sebowski

(Rushing in the classroom.)
Well, Mr. Brighton, well, well, well. I knew you had it in you.

Stone

Sebowski, go!

Sebowski

Yes, sir. *To Evan:* I'm watching you. *(Leaves smiling.)*

Stone

Let's go try to get through this.

Ruby, Evan, and Stone exit.

Act 2, Scene 4

Diedre

Did she just?

Margie

Just showing you what happened.

Diedre

But?

Margie

Yep

Diedre

And?

Margie

Uh-huh.

Diedre

Wow.

Margie

On a lighter note, class resumed as normal, and I was even asked to help out a little.

Evan

Okay, you guys take a seat somewhere. It's time that we get started. We're going to wait and rehearse "Tumble" after school today. Today in class we need to finish our Uta Hagen exercises. I need you to get with your partner and writes down the steps to your Destination scenario.

Ian enters from the back room with a bottle of water again.

Ian

Mr. B., Bryan's nearly as naked as a jaybird back in the costume room again.

Evan

(Walks to entrance of back room.) Bryan. You need to . . . (*Look of shock*). Whoa. Okay, Bryan. Cover up. Get your clothes back on. (*Evan has rest of conversation, looking away, uncomfortably.*)

Bryan's voice

Mr. Brighton, you know I don't mean anything by it. It's just comfortable. And it seems this is home, as many hours as I spend up here.

Evan

Bryan, it doesn't matter. That's enough. Dress yourself. (*Walking away,*
to himself.) Well, that'll be burned in my memory forever.

Evan walks to classroom door, looking out, spots Margie.

Evan

Margie! Margie, if you're not too busy, may I speak with you a minute?

Margie

Sure, Mr. B. What's up?

Evan

I have a young man in here, Bryan, who is a little too eager to go very close to *au naturale* in the costume room. I've talked to him many times. Do you think you could explain the female perspective and give him a short motherly talk about why such behavior is not appealing to the fairer sex?

Margie

Sure thing. Anything I can do to help.

Evan

(Re-entering the room.) Bryan!

Bryan enters, buttoning up his shirt, barefoot.

Bryan

Yes, sir. I can't find my flip-flops again.

Evan

They'll show up. Come here. I have someone who wants to speak with you.

Bryan

Is something wrong?

Evan

No. Just come out here.

They enter the hallway.

Evan

You know Ms. Margie, don't you?

Bryan

Sure. Hi, Ms. Margie.

Margie

Hello, Bryan.

Evan

Ms. Margie wants to talk with you for a few minutes.

Bryan

Okay.

They walk off together down the hall, out of sight, talking.

Evan re-enters the room.

Evan

So, do we all know what we're doing?

Jade enters dressed fit-to-kill, over-the-top super sexy.

Everyone stops and stares.

A few of the students whistle.

Evan

Jade, welcome to class. I'm not sure if our activities today are suited to your attire, but feel free to join in as you can.

Jade

(In a sexy voice) Thank you, Mr. Brighton.

She starts to move across the room. Olivia gives her non-verbal encouragement. She sits close to Logan.

Jade

May I sit here?

Logan

Sure

Jade

Do you have a partner, Logan?

Logan

Well, Vince and I are working together on this Destination scene.

Jade

Destination? Ah, yes. Sounds heavenly. Knowing where you're going and what you want.

Logan

Yeah.

Jade

What do you want, Logan? Do you know?

Logan

Huh?

Jade

Do you know what you want?

Logan

Not really. That's what we're working on.

Jade

Well, do you mind if I join your little group. I mean, three's not a crowd, is it?

Logan

Well, Vince and I . . .

Vince

It's okay with me. I don't mind.

Logan

(*Gives him a dirty look*) OK. I don't care. Join in.

Jade

Thank you, Logan. You're going to have to tell me what to do here, now. I don't understand all this stuff as much as you do.

Logan

Jade, you know this exercise forward and backward. You were working on it last Thursday. I saw you.

Jade

Well, I was just drawing from the inspiration in this room. I have a lot to learn from you.

Vince

Yeah.

Logan

(*to Vince*) Shut up.

Jade

So. Teach me, Logan.

Logan

Mr. B., I gotta go. I'll explain later.
(*He takes his backpack and leaves.*)

Jade is upset, sits back frustrated.

Vince

You still got me.

Jade

Shut up.

Olivia

(*approaching*) Jade.

Jade

Shut up.

Serena enters the room.

Evan

Oh, Serena. What a nice surprise. I didn't expect you so early
for the meeting. But to be honest, I didn't expect you at all really.
You know since the whole situation with Josh, I don't want you
to feel obligated to continue working with the department.

Serena

Mr. B. I do this because I want to. I wish Josh were here, but
even if can't be, I'm still part of what goes on here. I love these kids.

Evan

Understood. Thank you.

Margie and Bryan re-enter.

Margie

Now you know why we don't want to see that.

Bryan

I'm not doing it to *show* anybody.

Margie

I understand. But from a girl's perspective, you can see how
that might make a few of us uncomfortable?

Bryan

Yeah, I understand. Mr. B., I get it. I'll keep my magnificent body in my pants from now on. I don't want to offend.

Evan

Thank you. And thank you, Margie.

Margie

No problem. Off to clean the sinks in the girls' bathroom. Fun.

Evan

Bye.

Margie

Bye.

She exits and rejoins Diedre, watching.

The bell rings.

Evan

Okay, guys. We do have rehearsal today, but it's a late one. We're starting a bit later, about 5:30 so that you can take care of oil changes, bill paying, and shopping. I'll see you guys in a couple of hours.

#25--Background--Opening Up --MUSIC

They all say their good byes as they exit. Only Serena and Evan are in the room. It is obvious that she is nervous and he is worried.

Serena

So here we are.

Evan

Here we are.

Serena

What's wrong?

Evan

Oh, nothing. There is just so much on my mind, so much going on.

Serena

Is it the contest?

Evan

Well, that, yes. But a lot more.

Serena

Anything you care to talk about?

Evan

I really can't.

Serena

Oh.

Evan

Oh, don't take that wrong. I would LOVE to talk with someone, with . . . you, about it, but there are things I'm not allowed to discuss.

Serena

I understand. It's a lot harder to be a teacher than people realize.

Evan

Yeah, it is.

Serena

Especially when you work all the time.

Evan

Yeah

Serena

Especially when you care so much for your students.

Evan

Yeah.

Serena

Especially when you don't have anyone in your life you can share things with

Evan

Yeah.

Serena

Especially when you need someone special just to survive.

Evan

(*Slowly*) Yeah. (*He looks at her and for the first time feels something.*) Serena?

Serena

Yeah?

Evan

Is this?

Serena

Yeah.

Evan

Yeah.

Serena

Yeah

Evan

We have the vocabulary of some of the students.

Serena

Yeah

#26--IT IS YOU --SONG

EVAN

I NEVER THOUGHT THROUGH ALL MY YEARS IT COULD BE YOU I
NEVER SOUGHT WITH EYES OF LOVE TO LOOK FOR YOU.
I NEVER KNEW THE OPTION CLEAR...
IT'S AS IF MY HEART WERE SEARED, BUT...
I'M SO GLAD OH I'M SO GLAD THAT IS IT YOU.

SERENA

I NEVER KNEW WHEN SEEING YOU, THAT YOU WERE . . . HERE.
I NEVER FELT THE CARDS WERE DEALT WITH YOU.... HERE.
I NEVER FOUGHT WITHIN MY SOUL OVER FOOLISH THOUGHTS SO
BOLD

EVAN

ABOUT YOU, ABOUT YOU ABOUT YOU

SERENA

I NEVER KNEW THAT I WOULD FALL FOR ONE LIKE YOU

EVAN

I'D BRING THE SLIPPER FROM THE BALL TO ONE LIKE YOU I'D CLIMB
A MOUNTAIN TO ITS TOP,
I'M PRETTY SURE MY EARS WOULD POP, BUT
I'D DO IT IF IT MEANT THAT I'D FIND YOU.

SERENA

I ALWAYS HOPED THAT I WOULD LOVE. THEN THERE WAS ... YOU.

EVAN

NOW I CAN SHOUT TO STARS ABOVE THAT THERE IS YOU.

SERENA

NOW THERE WON'T BE A LONELY END.

EVAN

I'VE FOUND A LOVER AND A FRIEND.

BOTH

I'M SO GLAD, OH I'M SO GLAD, THAT IT IS YOU.
I'M SO GLAD, OH I'M SO GLAD, THAT IT IS YOU.

Song ends.

Diedre

Are you serious?

Margie

Yeah.

Diedre

I had no idea. That is so sweet!

Margie

Yeah.

Diedre

But she doesn't know about?

Margie

No

Diedre

What next?

Margie

We are close, so we are going to skip to the state contest!

Diedre

Already?

Margie

Yeah. They're at the capital now, there at the main university auditorium, you know, the big one. You've been there.

Diedre

Yeah.

Margie

And you know everybody comes, the principal, the booster club, all the family members.

Diedre

Yeah. Oh, all the family members? You mean Ruby Riley came?

Margie

For Magnus, she said.

Diedre

Um-hmm.

Margie

And a few unusual things happened.

Act 2, Scene 5

The group is backstage, excited and nervous.

Evan

Okay, guys, we're up in about twenty-five minutes. We have to get focused and ready. I'm proud of each you. Remember that we're a family, and . . .

Josh

(Running up) Bright!

Evan

Josh, what are you doing here? All the way here? We're about to go on.

Josh

I know. I know. Mr. Brighton. Listen. It wasn't true.

Evan

What?

Josh

The baby. It wasn't true. She was never pregnant. Her parents made her tell me. She'd been lying about the whole thing.

Melody

Are you serious?

Josh

Yeah. I mean, I'm kind of sad and all because I already loved the little fellow and was rearranging everything to suit him, but now I am like YEAH!

Evan

That's good to know, Josh. I am proud for you.

Josh

Is there any way?

Evan

What?

Josh

Bright. Is there any way? I can be in this show?

Evan

Now?

Josh

Now. I know every line.

Evan

That wouldn't be fair to TJ.

Josh

Yeah. I had to ask.

TJ

I understand.

Ruby

We'll it's good to see you didn't follow after Mr. Brighton's footprints after all.

Josh

What?

Evan

What?

Magnus

What are you talking about, Grandma?

Ruby

You mean you haven't told them, Mr. Brighton?

Evan

Ruby, what are you doing?

Ruby

I'm shocked that you haven't been bragging to everyone.

Evan

Ruby, this is neither the time or the place. We're about to go on stage at the state competition.

Serena

Time or place for what, Evan?

Ruby

You didn't even tell Ms. Joiner, Mr. Brighton? Why am I not surprised?

Evan

Why are you doing this?

Serena

Tell me what?

Ruby

Tell her, Mr. Brighton. Or would you rather it come from me?

Serena

What is she talking about.

Evan

Ms. Riley's daughter loved our plays and they inspired her to go to New York to try her hand at being an actress. While there, she met someone and moved to Paris. Ms. Riley claims to have gotten a letter from her long-lost daughter accusing me of violating her physically and mentally and that that is the reason she has left the US. Thanks to this new revelation, I'm under investigation.

Everyone reacts in shock.

Evan

There is not a word of it that is true, though.

Serena

Evan. (She runs away.)

The Stage Manager walks up.

Stage Manager

You have four minutes, Mr. Brighton.

Evan

Thank you.

Ruby

Good. There. People know you for who you are.

Vince

Bright, please tell me it's not true.

Evan

I promise, Vince. Not a word.

Ruby

I wouldn't believe a word he says.

TJ

I do.

Several Students

I do.

Magnus runs off.

Evan

Magnus!

Josh

Where'd my mom go?

Olivia

She ran off.

Josh

Ran off?

Evan

It's a long story.

Crystal

What are we going to go without Magnus?

Ruby laughs and walks off.

TJ

I'll do it.

Evan

What?

TJ

I'll do Magnus's part. I know it.

Evan

But what about . . . (*He looks at Josh.*) Yeah.

Josh

I'll do it.

Evan

Okay. We don't have any time to regroup. TJ, you're playing Ben, and Josh, you're Robert. We don't have time to do much. Just know this, guys: what you've heard has no bearing upon you. You're still the same as you were this morning. I can promise you I'm innocent, but even if I weren't, I'd still have faith in you. Go out there and show everyone what Legacy Road High School is made of! Who'll do a great job right now?

All Students

LEGACY ROAD WILL!

Evan

Places!

Contest Manager

(From off stage) And now, Legacy Road High School presents its original work, "Tumble."

Evan

(As they are leaving) I believe in you. *(Josh hugs him. TJ is the last to leave.)*

TJ

I believe in you.

Exits.

Act 2, Scene 6

#27--I TUMBLE ON THE ROAD –SONG

JOSH

I TUMBLE ON THE ROAD,
BUT I SEE THE BETTER GOAL
IT'S NOT WHAT I ACHIEVE.
IT'S WHAT IT'S MADE OF ME
I TUMBLE AND I STUMBLE
BUT I WOULDN'T CHANGE A THING
I'M PROUD OF THE JOURNEY
I'M HAPPY WITH THE VICTORY
BUT I'M HAPPIER BY FAR WITH THE PERSON
THIS JOURNEY'S MADE OF ME.

#28--THE MAIN TUMBLE SONG –SONG

"Tumble" A Ragtime number begins immediately. In this song, there is extensive choreography, a wide variety of dance moves

ALL

I TUMBLE ON THE ROAD TO CERTAINTY
I TUMBLE ON THE PATH TO PROSPERITY
I TUMBLE ON THE STREET TO IMMORTALITY
I TUMBLE ALL ALONG WITH WAY

MALES

AND WITH THE OTHER GUYS
WALKING BY
SINGING ALL THEIR LULLABIES
AND OVER AND AGAIN THEY DON'T SEE THE WAY

FEMALES

THEY WILL NOT SEE
CANNOT SEE
EVERYTHING SO CLEARLY
AND I KNOW
I SEE THE LIGHT
I KNOW I USE MY MIGHT
I TRY TO FIGHT AND FIGHT FOR WHAT IT RIGHT

ALL

AND WHERE THE OTHER GUYS
STUMBLE, ALL LOSING THEIR WAY
THEY STUMBLE AND FUMBLE
NOT KNOWING WHAT TO SAY

I CHOOSE A TUMBLE
A GENTLY FALL TO HELP ME ON MY WAY
AND WHEN I'M LYING THERE

THINKING THERE
TRYING THERE
BLINKING THERE
CRYING THERE
SINKING THERE
DYING THERE
STINKING THERE
SIGHING THERE
WINKING THERE
I KNOW THAT I CAN GET UP FOR I CHOSE TO FALL DOWN
I CAN GET UP FOR I CHOSE TO STALL DOWN
I CAN GET UP AND THEN GO MY MERRY WAY!

Big applause!

Act 2, Scene 7

Students return backstage to the wind-down room, all excited.

Evan

Oh my Gosh! You guys were amazing!

Everyone is talking and excited.

Stone

(Enters.) Students, excellent work. You made Legacy High proud once again, no matter the outcome.

Evan

Thank you, Mr. Stone. I'm quite proud of them.

Ruby and Sebowski enter, both upset.

Ruby

I have no idea how they went on and . . . *(She sees Mr. Stone.)* Oh, hello, Mr. Stone.

Stone

Hello, Ms. Riley.

Sebowski

Hello, Mr. Stone. So, Mr. Brighton, you did it again. I would enjoy these few minutes.

Stone

That's enough, Mr. Sebowski.

Magnus enters with Cynthia and her friend, Edmond Charles.

Ruby

Cynthia!

Cynthia

Hello, Mother.

Ruby

Cynthia.

Evan

Cynthia Riley

Cynthia

Hello, Mr. Brighton.

Magnus

Mr. Stone, my mother has something to tell you.

Ruby

Cynthia, it's been years. We need to talk. How did you get here? Why are you? What's the . . . ?

Magnus

That can wait, Grandma. Mom, tell him.

Cynthia

I heard there's a letter with my name on it having something to do with Mr. Evan Brighton.

Evan

There is, indeed.

Cynthia

Well, I want you to know that that letter didn't come from me.

All the students react happily.

Cynthia

Mr. Brighton was nothing but a perfect gentleman to me.

Stone

I figured as much.

Sebowski

This proves nothing!

Stone

Enough, Mr. Sebowski.

Josh runs off, unseen by Evan.

Ruby

Cynthia.

Cynthia

Mother, why would you do that? Why would you try to destroy this man and these kids?

Ruby

It has nothing to do with these kids. But . . . I hadn't heard from you in so long and . . .

Cynthia

Did you ever wonder that there may be a reason for that?

Ruby

But . . .

Cynthia

I knew what was happening with Magnus.

Ruby

What?

Cynthia

Yes, I kept up with Magnus, sent him money, cards.

Ruby

What? *(looks at Magnus)*

Cynthia

Any extra money he had, to pay for food and help with bills? That came from me.

Ruby

I always figured he stole money.

Cynthia

No, I shouldn't have left him with you. For that, I apologize. I begged him to move to England with me a couple of years ago, but he begged *me* to let him stay at Legacy Road, to finish out his high school years with the company. I knew if you weren't out any money, you'd never even notice he was there.

Ruby

England? What about France?

Cynthia

Mother, I never moved to France. I went to England and met Edmond here, Edmond Charles, my husband.

Ruby

Husband?

Stone

Mr. Brighton, the investigation is over. Congratulations.

Sebowski

This man is still a menace! You should tell him . . .

Stone

You're fired.

Sebowski

Exactly.

Stone

No, *you're* fired, Mr. Sebowski. I'm tired of your constant insults and harassment. You can leave now.

Sebowski

Wait a minute!

Stone

Please leave before I call the university police from their coffee stations.

Sebowski

You haven't heard the last of Anton Sebowski. You'll be hearing from my attorney before you return to your ugly little, poorly decorated office. (*Leaves.*)

Logan

I hate that guy.

Magnus

I'm so sorry, Mr. Brighton. Please don't hate me.

Ruby sneaks out.

Evan

You brought your mom here and cleared my name. How could I hate you?

Magnus

Well, she and Edmond came to watch my senior contest play. I wasn't going to tell my Grandma until I had to. When all those lies came out, I knew I had to do something. I'm sorry I missed the show.

Evan

Don't worry. We covered it well.

Josh enters with Serena, looking a little sheepish.

Evan

There you two are!

Josh

I told mom what happened, that it was a big lie. There she is, mom, Magnus's mom all the way from Europe. From Europe? Wait a minute? How did?

Magnus

Long story. I'll catch you up later.

#29--IT IS YOU REPRISE –SONG

Serena

I'm so sorry. It wasn't that I didn't believe you. It was just too much to take in.

Evan

I understand.

Serena

I feel like such a fool.

Evan

Nonsense. That was a lot to deal with. But I promise it was all rubbish.

Serena

I know, and I should have known that. I know you.

Evan

And I know you.

SERENA
(SINGING BEGINS.)

I ALWAYS HOPED THAT I WOULD LOVE. THEN THERE WAS ... YOU.

EVAN

NOW I CAN SHOUT TO STARS ABOVE THAT THERE IS YOU.

SERENA

NOW THERE WON'T BE A LONELY END.

EVAN

I'VE FOUND A LOVER AND A FRIEND.

BOTH

I'M SO GLAD, OH I'M SO GLAD, THAT IT IS YOU.
I'M SO GLAD, OH I'M SO GLAD, THAT IT IS YOU.

Vince kisses Crystal. She is in shock, then kisses him back.

Everyone cheers.

#30--JOURNEY TO SOMEWHERE REPRISE –SONG

ALL

THEN I KNOW, I KNOW I AM HERE
THOUGH I STILL HAVE MANY DOUBTS AND FEARS
I WILL STILL DO MY BEST TO SEE THE RAINBOW
THROUGH THE PRISM OF MY TEARS?

OH, I KNOW, I KNOW HOW IMPORTANT IT IS TO BE
A PERSON OF INTEGRITY
ON MY WAY HERE.

Stage Manager walks in.

Stage Manager

We'll have the results for the whole contest in about two hours
in the Grand Ballroom. You are welcome to head over there
and wait in your allotted section.

Evan

Thank you.

Stage Manager

By the way, do any of you know a woman named Ruby? Is she
with this group?

Magnus

Yes, she's my grandma. Why?

Stage Manager

She just wandered on stage during a strike, fell off the stage, and
it seems she . . . broke her leg. She's cursing and yelling and
appears to be screaming out her own name, arguing with . . .
herself. We have an ambulance on its way.

Everyone scrambles out.

Act 2, Scene 8

#31--Background--After the Awards –MUSIC

Margie

And then after the awards ceremony . . .

Diedre

After??

Margie

Just watch

They all walk outside, many with trophies.

Evan

We didn't get every award we wanted, but we racked up.

Vince

Yes, we did.

Crystal

Congrats, Mr. Best Song and Score!

Vince

Thank you, Ms. Outstanding Actress.

Crystal

Gracias. But the big congrats goes to the Best Actor in the state, Mr. Josh Gardner and to Outstanding Actor in a Small Role, Mr. TJ Keller.

Josh

Thanks

TJ

Yeah, thanks.

Evan

Congrats to all you guys. We were Second overall, but that's not bad at all.

Stone

Not at all.

Caroline approaches.

Evan

Caroline, I didn't know you were here.

Caroline

I wouldn't miss my kids for anything. Come hug me, youngsters.

Several of them hug her.

Caroline

I'm sorry I didn't see the actual awards ceremony. I was busy "hob-snobbing" with all those snobs, well, my friends. (*Laughs*) I hadn't seen the president of Harrington since Christmas and the chancellor of the state university since my birthday party last year. I heard about the trophies, though. I am so happy.

Magnus, Edmond, and Cynthia walk up.

Evan

How's Ms. Riley?

Cynthia

She broke her leg all right, snapped it right in two. They're keeping her overnight for observation, though. We're going to go check on her before we go to our hotel.

Magnus

I see the trophies!

Vince

Yep, yep!

Magnus

Olivia called me and told me who got what. That's great! I'm happy, Mr. B. Sorry I missed it all.

Evan

It's okay, Magnus.

Magnus

I have some good news, though.

Serena

I don't know if I can handle much more.

Magnus

Tell them, Mom.

Cynthia

Well, my husband here owns controlling interest in a little theatre called the Mercury right off of Shaftesbury Avenue in a little neighborhood in London called the West End.

Students begin to gasp.

Cynthia

And he would like to know if . . . (*She looks at Edmond.*)

Edmond

Your work was outstanding today, and would love to invite you to perform "Tumble" as our special guests for week's engagement at the Mercury. And I would like a chance to see my stepson onstage sometime.

Students begin to scream, everyone happy.

Edmond

However, there's a catch.

Evan

A catch?

Edmond

I can supply you the house and the audience, but you have figure out some way to get there. International travel for a large group is rather expensive.

Evan

Oh.

T
he students act disappointed.

Stone

Evan, as much as I'd like to jump in and say the school could pay for it, there's no way. We're talking about a lot of money, a whole lot of money. I'm so sorry.

Evan

We're so very honored to receive the invitation, Mr. Charles. We would love to come and perform, but I'm afraid we're going to have to decline.

Caroline

Why?

Evan

We'd have to do the show before some of these kids graduate--
soon. And we can't get the money to fly twenty-five people to
London and to put them up for a week.

Caroline

Yes, you can.

Evan

Yes, I can what?

Caroline

Get the money.

Evan

No, I can't.

Caroline

You already have it.

Evan

Where?

Carolyn

Here. I'll pay for it.

Evan

What?

Carolyn

I'll pay for it.

Evan

Carolyn, can you . . .?

Carolyn

Sure, darling, it's no big deal. What I can give to *you*, I don't have to give the *government*. Figure up the total, and I'll write you a check. You guys have places to go!

Evan

Are you sure?

Carolyn

Quite sure.

Evan

But in the past when we've needed things . . .

Carolyn

You never asked.

Evan

Oh. (*Looks at Mr. Stone*) Mr. Stone?

Stone

I'd have to run it by Ms. Vanderschmidt and the board of trustees, but, in the past, if the finances have been there, the "powers that be" have always approved such opportunities. As far as I know, the answer is . . . (*looks around at the students*) yes. Congratulations, students, it seems you'll be representing Legacy Road High in London!

The students cheer.

Jade walks up to Logan.

Jade

Okay. I have to know. I have thrown myself at you unashamedly. Why don't you like me?

Logan

I never said I don't like you.

Jade

But you're not interested?

Logan

Jade

Jade

Right?

Logan

Right.

Jade

Why?

Logan

Jade

Jade

Why?

Logan

(Keeping his voice low) Because . . .

Jade

Because why?

Logan

Because I'm . . .

Jade

You're what?

Logan

I'm . . . asexual.

Jade

(*Loudly*) You're . . . asexual?!

Logan

(*Sarcastically—as if saying "You just shouted my business to the world."*)
Thanks.

Everyone looks at him in shock.

Jade

You're . . . What exactly does that mean?

Logan

Jade.

Jade

You're asexual?

Logan

That means that I'm just not interested in . . . I mean in general,
I'm not . . .

Jade

I know what it means.

Logan

Well, good. I suppose. (*Looks around uncomfortably.*)

Jade

And I? Oh. That makes sense.

Logan

(Still with sarcasm Jade doesn't acknowledge)
Glad I could help.

Jade

I see everything now.

Logan

You're welcome.

Jade

No hard feelings?

Logan

Other than . . . (*Looks around. Deep breath.*) No.

Jade hugs him and leaves.

Jade

(to Olivia) He's "asexual." I still have it.

Vince

(to Logan) You're asexual?

Logan

I'm . . . well, I'm . . . yeah.

Vince

Okay.

Logan

Okay?

Vince

Okay.

Evan

(to Serena) Today, everything changes. You know, I've held on to a lot of pain that no one knows about. There are chapters in my life that will always be a part of who I am, but those chapters are in the past. Today's about new beginnings. Things may not have turned out how I expected them to, but they turned out. And I could never even dream that I'be right here, right now. And to be honest, I'm happy it turned out this way. The choices we make today determine the places we end up tomorrow.

Serena

Yeah. *(Smiles)*

They kiss. The students cheer.

Evan

(to the students) Success isn't just about victory, guys.

All the Students

It's about integrity.

Epilogue

Margie

So, there you have it.

Diedre

That was quite a ride.

Margie

You're telling me. Most of it, I saw. Some of it, I got from reliable sources, but in every case, that's what happened.

Diedre

What happened to all these folks?

#32--I'VE NEVER SEEN A SKY SO BRIGHT REPRISE -- SONG

Margie

Well, Mr. Sebowski now works for the state as a contest manager. Ms. Riley is walking again, but she opted for an early retirement instead of facing libel charges. Several of the kids are at various colleges from UCLA to Julliard. A few are in movies, a couple are on Off-Broadway, and Vince is working in the West End.

Diedre

That's great.

Margie

Evan and Serena are getting married soon.

Diedre

Aw.

Margie

Yep. And he gets at least ten legitimate job offers every single year. I have a feeling, he'll take one soon. Until then, I plan on keeping on enjoying these kids and their shows. You know, people come and go out of our daily lives, kids graduate, people move on, but it never has to truly end. You can keep the connection if you really want to! You should always remember being part of something great. Never dismiss it. Always cherish it. It'll be over before the blink of an eye. We're made of memories. Never be ashamed of them. It's not until a time in our life is over that we really, really wish we could step back and hear someone yell . . .

ENTIRE CAST

PLACES!

The whole cast enters and sings.

ALL

CHORUS
I'VE NEVER SEEN THE SKY SO BRIGHT
I'VE NEVER SEEN THE SUN PUT OUT SUCH LIGHT
I'VE NEVER SEEN A DAY SO FULL OF PROMISE AND OF HOPE
I'VE NEVER SEEN A WORLD SO NEW
I'VE NEVER SEEN MY PROBLEMS BE SO FEW
I'VE NEVER SEEN A SKY, I'VE NEVER SEEN A SKY SO BRIGHT.

(BRIDGE)
IF I LIVED A MILLION YEARS OR MORE,
IF I FOUND THE SPOILS OF ANCIENT WARS,
IF I HAPPENED ON THE MYSTERIES OF ALL BEING AND OF TIME,
IF I LEARNED THE WISDOM OF THE SAGE,
READ EVERY WORD ON EVERY PAGE,
I'D NEVER FIND THE PEACE I FEEL JUST WAKING UP TODAY.

ALL

(CHORUS)
I'VE NEVER SEEN THE SKY SO BRIGHT
I'VE NEVER SEEN THE SUN PUT OUT SUCH LIGHT
I'VE NEVER SEEN A DAY SO FULL OF PROMISE AND OF HOPE
I'VE NEVER SEEN A WORLD SO NEW
I'VE NEVER SEEN MY PROBLEMS BE SO FEW
I'VE NEVER SEEN A SKY,
I'VE NEVER SEEN A SKY SO BRIGHT.

#33--Background--Bows –MUSIC

End of Show

Lowery Christopher Collins (Chris) has been an educator and writer for over thirty years. He is currently a professor of English at Panola College in Carthage, Texas. He has taught at the high school, middle school, and elementary school levels and as an English and literature instructor at the college and university level. For several years, he was a high school theatre director and a gifted education consultant. He's been honored with several teaching awards, including the Young Audiences of Northeast Texas Outstanding Service to the Profession Award and the Kennedy Center's Steven Sondheim Award for being one of the most "Inspirational Teachers" in the U.S.

He is also an award-winning playwright of over thirty scripts, a weekly newspaper columnist, a short story writer, a poet, a pianist, a vocalist, a songwriter, a recording artist with Daywind Studios, the founder and artistic director of Stagelands Theatre Company, an aspiring novelist, and a (former) choir director. He's taught a variety of classes, from rhetoric and composition to literature to acting to the Bible.

He holds a Bachelor of Arts Degree in English and History and a Master of Arts Degree in English from Stephen F. Austin State University in Texas and has served on fine arts and gifted education committees as well as on a board of governors for a small playhouse.

In addition to his interests in teaching, directing, and writing, he has a fondness for lighthouses, windmills, filmmaking, salsa, sculpture, Flannery O'Connor, travel, dominos, guacamole, social media, genetics, Maine, landscaping, pillows, gospel music, Shakespeare, marbles, YouTube, quantum physics, movies, weird jokes, maps, trees, cold rooms, and Texas.

He can be reached at mrchriscollins@hotmail.com,

on Facebook at www.facebook.com/tofferdreams,

on Twitter at "tofferdreams,"

and at his website: www.ChristopherCollinsOnline.com.

To view Christopher Collins's books and other writing, visit Ponderlake Publishing, at www.ponderlake.com.